THE OUTLA⬛⬛⬛⬛⬛⬛⬛⬛⬛⬛⬛⬛⬛⬛GUN.

Longarm slash⬛⬛⬛⬛⬛⬛⬛⬛⬛⬛⬛⬛⬛⬛⬛The
outlaw's pistol⬛⬛⬛⬛⬛⬛⬛⬛⬛⬛⬛⬛⬛⬛his
skull cracked li⬛⬛⬛⬛⬛⬛⬛⬛⬛g him instantly.
The other outlaws sat up fast, reaching for their guns.
Feeling more comfortable at close range with a pistol,
Longarm dropped the rifle and made his cross draw.
Six-gun in hand, he concentrated on making every
shot count. A bullet grazed his temple and sent his
hat flying. Longarm staggered and shot the last outlaw twice, knocking him over backwards . . .

DON'T MISS THESE
ALL-ACTION WESTERN SERIES
FROM THE BERKLEY PUBLISHING GROUP

THE GUNSMITH by J. R. Roberts
Clint Adams was a legend among lawmen, outlaws, and ladies. They called him . . . the Gunsmith.

LONGARM by Tabor Evans
The popular long-running series about U.S. Deputy Marshal Long—his life, his loves, his fight for justice.

SLOCUM by Jake Logan
Today's longest-running action Western. John Slocum rides a deadly trail of hot blood and cold steel.

BUSHWHACKERS by B. J. Lanagan
An action-packed series by the creators of Longarm! The rousing adventures of the most brutal gang of cutthroats ever assembled—Quantrill's Raiders.

TABOR EVANS

LONGARM

AND THE FOUR CORNERS GANG

JOVE BOOKS, NEW YORK

LONGARM AND THE FOUR CORNERS GANG

A Jove Book / published by arrangement with
the author

PRINTING HISTORY
Jove edition / November 1999

The Penguin Putnam Inc. World Wide Web site address is
http://www.penguinputnam.com

ISBN: 0-515-12687-X

A JOVE BOOK®
Jove Books are published by The Berkley Publishing Group,
a division of Penguin Putnam Inc.,
375 Hudson Street, New York, New York 10014.
JOVE and the "J" design
are trademarks belonging to Penguin Putnam Inc.

PRINTED IN THE UNITED STATES OF AMERICA

10 9 8 7 6 5 4 3 2 1

Chapter 1

Deputy Marshal Custis Long was on an overdue vacation in Flagstaff, Arizona, where both the weather and the scenery were magnificent. He was stretched out in a big canvas hammock slung from a pair of tall pines located behind the Big Elk Lodge with a beer in one hand and a cigar in the other. Custis wore a smile on his handsome face and stared up at the huge puffy clouds that floated just to the west of the San Francisco peaks. How long had it been since he'd actually had a *real* vacation? Four years, or was it five? Longarm didn't want to think about it. What was the point when he had another three whole weeks to do nothing but soak up the sun and the scent of the pines?

Custis was bare-chested and felt more relaxed than he had in years. His boss, Marshal Billy Vail, had not been pleased about his favorite deputy being out of service for the entire month of August. However, to Longarm's way of thinking, Billy was never happy since he'd traded his freedom for a desk at the federal building in Denver and a promotion into the ranks of overpaid paper pushers. Longarm felt a little sorry for Marshal Vail, but he figured that when a man collected a wife and kids it was inevitable that he become domesticated and desk bound. That's why Longarm was determined to remain a bachelor and a deputy

1

working out in the field on important crimes. But sometimes all the hard lonely travel, the danger, and the poor meals could turn a fella's thoughts toward settling down and accepting the marriage yoke. And, if . . .

"Yoo-hoo, Custis, darling!"

Longarm turned his head slightly to the left. The overhanging pines and the big puffy clouds could wait a while, because now one of the best things about Flagstaff was just about to reappear.

"Custis, honey pie!"

"I'm over here, Hilda!"

"Oh," she said, emerging from around the trees that hid him from view of the lodge, "are you hiding from me, you big, handsome devil!"

"Not a chance!"

Longarm wasn't kidding, because Hilda was very easy on the eyes. Blondhaired and blue eyed with plump, dimpled cheeks, she was endowed with large bouncing breasts. Fun loving and humorous, Hilda possessed a laugh that rivaled mountain thunder and a lustiness that was rare indeed. Her last name was Swenson, and she was second-generation Swedish. Twice married and looking for a third prize, Hilda had probably worn out her former husbands in bed just as she was wearing Longarm down to a nubbin. But shoot, if a man couldn't satisfy a passionate woman— no matter how energetic and aggressive—for a mere month, well, it was time for him to hang up his spurs.

"So there you are!" Hilda cried, hurrying over to Longarm's side and bending over to kiss his lips. "What a lazybones you are!"

"Like I told you," he replied, "when I work, I work hard. When I relax, I'm good at that, too. And when I make love, well, I rarely hear any complaints."

"And you'll not be hearing any from me, big boy!" She knelt beside the hammock and winked. "Want to have a little fun?"

"With you, sure!" Longarm poked his cigar into the

2

neck of his beer bottle and closed his eyes as the buxom woman unbuttoned his pants and began to massage his hard, flat stomach and his thickening manhood.

"Hilda?"

"Yeah?"

"Aren't you afraid that your boss will come looking for you?"

"No."

"But if he did and you lost your job because he's sort of prudish . . ."

"Ah," she said, with that big, toothy smile, "he needs me more than I need him. Who else is going to clean the rooms so good and so fast?"

"I don't know."

"Nobody, that's who!"

Longarm had only known Hilda since the day he'd arrived at the lodge, but he'd soon learned that it was impossible to argue with her on any level. Once Hilda had a course of action or an idea locked firmly in mind, you might as well try to turn a river's tide as to change her intentions. So he laced his fingers behind the back of his head, closed his eyes, and let Hilda do what she wanted.

"Oh my," she giggled, "you are such a *big* fellow! And so tasty, too!"

Longarm sighed with contentment as Hilda took his manhood into her mouth and began sucking on it like a stick of peppermint candy. "Hilda," he drawled, "you have a one-track mind."

She mumbled something unintelligible, and Longarm's toes curled as the woman expertly worked over his throbbing rod. He lost track of time, and his hips began to move involuntarily as Hilda also became more and more excited.

"Hey," he panted, "I think I've had about as much of this as I can stand."

"That is good," she told him as she hiked up her dress to reveal that she wore no underclothes. "I still have a few rooms to clean, so we don't have all day, you know."

3

"Yeah, but we've been going at it every night and I'm—"

Longarm didn't get to finish because Hilda laughed and jumped on top of him, impaling herself on his slick rod. She cried out with pleasure, and then they heard the canvas tear under their combined weight.

"Oh my . . ."

Before Longarm could say another word, the hammock separated in the center and flipped them upside down. They landed with Longarm on top. Hilda's eyes dilated and she gasped as Longarm plunged to new depths in her womanhood.

"Oh, my goodness!" she cried, grabbing his buttocks with both hands so that he could not move. "No man has been so far in me before!"

Longarm wanted to laugh because her blue eyes were the size of silver dollars. "Well, how do you like it?"

"I *love* it!" she cried, locking her powerful legs around the small of his back and thrusting hard.

Longarm was pretty dry because of Hilda's insatiable demands, but he had never been one to quit, so he lunged up and down until he felt the fire, and he exploded just as Hilda's voice changed and she shuddered and clawed his back, which was already scratched all to hell.

"Take it easy!" he cried, as Hilda thrashed and clawed in the throes of ecstasy.

In a few moments, her body went limp, and they lay gasping on the pine needles, gazing up at the ruined hammock.

"Your boss is gonna be pretty upset about this and blame me."

"Ah," she said, "you just tell him that it must have been a bear that tried to take a nap in his hammock."

"A bear?"

"Sure! He's afraid of bears and blames them for all sorts of things. You being a marshal and all, he'll believe you."

Longarm shook his head. "I can't hardly imagine that

4

anyone would believe a *bear* would try to take a nap in a hammock. But, if that's what you suggest, then that's what I'll tell him.''

"It will work. He's from Philadelphia and will believe anything you say.''

Longarm extracted himself from Hilda's powerful clutches and retrieved his beer, but it was all spilled out. The cigar was fine, so he jammed it back between his teeth and buckled up his pants.

Hilda lowered her dress and said, "So, maybe I get away for a little more fun later, huh?''

"Listen, I sort of need to rest a while.''

"Rest? What else have you been doing all week?''

"You mean when we weren't doing it?''

"Sure!''

"Well, I can't hardly remember because that's about all we've done. Don't you ever get tired?''

"Me? Tired?'' Hilda threw out her big chest and laughed. "Listen,'' she said, "when I find a man like you, I don't like to waste so much time.''

"I see.''

"I go clean those other rooms now and tell Mr. Voss that a bear tried to sleep in his hammock and it split. When you see him, you tell him you *saw* the bear and it was very large and lazy. Like a man I know!''

Hilda went off laughing, and Longarm shook his head. He studied the hammock and knew that it couldn't be repaired. Too bad. It had been his favorite place to relax, and he'd enjoyed the solitude of the surrounding pines. He'd also considered it a hiding place from Hilda, who was quickly wearing him down to nothing. Why, he'd bet he'd lost ten pounds, all of it while humping that remarkable woman!

Longarm went back to his room and napped for an hour, then he went to the office and told Mr. Voss about seeing the bear in the hammock. It wasn't easy because he couldn't imagine that anyone would believe such a ridiculous story, but Voss did.

"It's too bad," the lodge manager said. "I will order a new hammock tomorrow."

"Any chance that it would come in the next couple of days?"

"No, I'm afraid not."

"I'm sorry to hear that."

"I have a telegram for you from Denver."

Longarm frowned, knowing that his boss was the only one who knew his whereabouts and that Billy might have a job for him that couldn't wait.

"Why don't you hang onto the telegram for a while," he replied. "Like about three more weeks."

Voss was a tall, thin man in his fifties who wore thick, wire-rimmed spectacles. He looked very scholarly, and Longarm could not imagine why he had gotten into this line of work for which he seemed so unsuited. "You want me to hold it for *three weeks*?"

"I was only kidding," Longarm replied, taking the telegram and slipping it into his pocket. When he returned to his room, he'd toss it in the trash and put the matter out of his mind.

Hilda found him snoozing at about six that evening and climbed into bed with him. "Let's get at it, big boy!"

Longarm groaned. "I'm feeling a little weak and hungry," he complained. "Why don't we go to town and have dinner, and then later we can do it again."

"I have a better idea," Hilda said. "Let's do it now *and* after dinner!"

Longarm tried to spring out of bed and give himself time to make an excuse, but Hilda was all over him before he could make his move. And, sure enough, they were at it again in a few minutes, and damned if it wasn't good!

Afterward, as Longarm lay limp and completely exhausted with fresh scratches on his back, he whispered, "Hilda, I have a confession to make."

"Yeah?"

"Yeah. I need to rest up and restore my essence."

"Your what?"

"Essence. You know, my juices. I'm running dry."

She giggled and jabbed him hard in the ribs. "I don't think so," she said. "Your 'juices' still feel pretty good to me."

"A man who goes to the well too often can go dry," Longarm tried to explain. "It's like . . . well, a cow. You can't milk it every couple of hours."

"You're no cow!"

"Of course not. But, well, I'm running dry."

She tweaked his cheek and said, "Let Hilda be the judge of that. Okay?"

Longarm knew it was useless to argue. "You got anything more for my poor back?"

"Roll over and I'll take a look."

He rolled over.

"Oh," Hilda sighed, "I did it again, didn't I!"

"You sure did." Longarm wasn't pleased. "And dammit, I'm going to put gloves on you the next time. At this rate, I'll bleed to death in the next few weeks."

"So much complaining today," Hilda said, pouting. "Maybe I should find a *young* and *fresh* lover."

Longarm was almost tempted to agree, but Hilda's breasts were about the most beautiful he'd ever seen and, well, he was having an unbelievably good time. If only he could slow Hilda down to just three or four times a day, then it would be perfect.

"Listen," he said, "why don't you put some salve on my back, and when the bleeding stops, we'll go out and get a couple of steaks in town?"

"I would like that," she said, brightening. "I'll go put on a clean dress and fix my hair."

"Good. But do my back first, all right? I can't stand to lose any more blood."

"Oh sure, big boy!" she laughed. "I will fix."

7

When he was alone, Longarm climbed weakly off the bed and staggered over to the mirror. He tried to get a look at his lacerated back but couldn't, and that was probably for the better. Hilda was a wildcat, and he'd be damned if he wouldn't buy her a pair of gloves when they went into town this evening.

Longarm was so exhausted he nearly fell asleep at the dinner table. Hilda got even more upset when he begged off their lovemaking and shoved her out the door so he could finally get a full night's rest. He was starting to think that, maybe—just maybe—it would be nice to spend the last week in Santa Fe where he knew a few lovely senoritas who were affectionate in comparison to Hilda.

Because of his back, he had to sleep on his stomach, which wasn't his style, so he tossed restlessly until late and then finally got disgusted with himself and went outside to admire the stars. Afterward, Custis trudged over to his trash can and extracted the telegram he'd received from Billy. Straightening it out on his bedside table, he fired his lamp and read the following:

Dear Custis: I'm afraid there is an emergency that cannot be ignored and for which no other man in the field is as well qualified to handle. Furthermore, the emergency is taking place in Arizona, and you are the only good choice.

"Here we go again," Longarm said, knowing he ought to find a match and incinerate the telegram before reading another word. But Longarm's curiosity got the best of him, so he cussed himself out a little and continued reading.

The emergency that I am referring to concerns a gang of murderers and thieves who are terrorizing the train and stagecoaches about a hundred miles east of Flagstaff. Reports state that they are also murdering and looting up near the Four Corners badland coun-

8

try. Only yesterday, three passengers were shot to death on the Santa Fe and several women were assaulted in a manner unfit for me to describe. Deputy Long, you have always been a man who both appreciates and respects women and who cannot abide their misuse. In short, you are a true gentlemen, while also being an admirer of the gentler sex. Because of this, I appeal to you to cut your vacation short and bring the Four Corners Gang to justice. There is no other man I can turn to in this emergency. Thank you, and when the job is done, you need only simply return to your extended vacation. Now, what could be fairer?

Longarm balled the telegram up and pitched it into the wastebasket with a snort of disgust. It was typical Billy Vail talk, meaning that the facts were greatly exaggerated. No doubt someone had robbed the train and perhaps had even insulted a woman. Longarm figured that Billy was simply trying to save the agency some travel money and take advantage of his being in Flagstaff.

"Not a chance," he muttered, blowing out the bedside lamp and trying again to go to sleep.

Longarm awoke early, dressed and then slipped out before Hilda could arrive and do what she most loved to do. It was only a short walk into Flagstaff, and Longarm went straight to the local marshal's office, where he introduced himself to a pudgy man of about forty who seemed a lot more interested in reading about the train robbery than solving it.

"So what really happened?" Longarm asked, pulling up a chair and wishing Marshal Potter would invite him to pour himself a cup of coffee.

"There were five of them, and they wore masks," Potter drawled. "So no one ever saw their faces, but it's the same ones that have struck the train over and over again. They've also robbed stagecoaches and raped a rancher's wife and daughter over in the Painted Desert country to the north-east.''

''I never heard of this.''

''Well, I never heard of you,'' Potter replied. ''And anyway, it's a local matter.''

''Not if the robbers took federal money or mail.''

Potter grunted.

''Well,'' Longarm demanded to know. ''Did they?''

''Sure they did! They stole every damn thing that was worth anything. Robbed all the passengers and even the train crew. Blew the safe. Took the money and the mail. Had their pleasure with some of the women passengers they dragged into the mail car while they was robbin' it.''

''Then, why haven't you formed a posse and gotten after them?''

''Hey,'' Potter said, ''you may be a big man in Denver, but you ain't nothing special in Flag. So back off and simmer down!''

''Answer my question.'' Longarm was on his feet now and towering over Potter, who was beginning to look nervous.

''Well, to begin with, I'm paid by the townsfolk and businessmen of Flag, and they wouldn't much want me to go off and leave them unprotected.''

''That's it?'' Longarm asked with amazement. ''You won't go after those outlaws because you don't want to leave the comforts of this town!''

''That *ain't* what I just said.''

''What kind of law officer are you?'' Longarm demanded. ''How can you allow this gang of murderers, thieves and rapists to go free when they operate so near to your town? And doesn't the rancher whose wife and daughter were raped mean anything to you?''

Potter was getting red in the face. ''They was just Navajos who don't pay no taxes or help pay my wages.''

Something in Longarm snapped. He reached out, grabbed the marshal by the shirtfront, and hauled him completely

10

out of his chair. " 'Just Navajos'!" he shouted. "My gawd, they were women!"

Potter started to shake. "You . . . you better let go of me and simmer down," he stammered. "You can't treat a fellow lawman this way!"

Longarm hurled the marshal into his chair with such force that Potter did a complete somersault and landed on his head. He howled in fear and then crabbed under his desk screaming, "I'll have you arrested for assault! I'll have your badge, Marshal Long!"

"Well by gawd, when I think that you and I are in the same profession it almost makes me ashamed to wear a badge," Longarm raged as he marched to the door and shot outside, knocking a couple of eavesdroppers over.

He went straight to the newspaper office and barged inside, shouting, "Who is the managing editor?"

There were only two men in the office, and the older of the pair stepped forward looking very worried. "Mister, if I printed something that upset you, I sure do apologize. It's only human to make mistakes, but heavenly to forgive so . . ."

"Listen," Longarm interrupted, managing to curb his fury, "I'm not here to settle a score for anything you wrote."

"You're not?"

"No."

"Then why are you so upset, Mister?"

Longarm wasted no words of explanation. When he was finished, he said, "I'd like to read every account you've printed of these attacks and robberies."

"Why, of course, Marshal. And I certainly don't blame you for being upset with that sorry excuse for a marshal that we have in office."

"How'd he get elected?"

"His father owns the bank, and a lot of people *owe* that bank."

"Well," Longarm said, "that is no excuse."

11

"I know," the editor agreed, introducing himself as Mr. Evans. "But Joseph Potter also owns three saloons and buys everyone who votes for his son drinks on the house, come election day. Between those two powerful leverages, his son regularly gets elected."

"That's pathetic!"

"I couldn't agree more."

"Have you written editorials denouncing his lack of professionalism and willingness to do his sworn duty?"

"I have," Evans replied. "And people fully agree. However, when it comes time to vote, they seem to forget their principles and . . . well, we do have a problem."

Longarm shook his head. "Let's see those articles."

"Are you thinking of going after the Four Corners Gang?" Evans asked hopefully.

"It's possible."

"If you are successful in their apprehension, Marshal Long, this town would be very much in your debt."

"Just get me the articles and leave me alone for a while until I get some idea of what kind of men they are."

"Animals," Evans said flatly. "Wild and depraved animals whose faces no man has seen while they commit their heinous acts. Then they vanish into the Painted Desert and the Indian country like ghosts."

"How do you know that, if they haven't been chased?"

"There is a bounty on their heads. A sizable bounty paid by one of our leading citizens because his wife was . . . well, you'll read all about it in the paper."

"And even with the bounty, no one has had any luck?"

Evans turned his palms upward in a gesture of futility. "Who knows?" he replied. "Anyone and everyone who has tried to capture or kill those three have simply vanished."

"Vanished?"

"That's right," the editor said, "at least a dozen men that I know of have never returned from the Indian country.

12

If the outlaws didn't kill them, the waterless desert or the Navajo probably did.''

Longarm opened his mouth to speak, then clamped it shut and waited to read what he might soon be up against.

Perhaps, he thought, Billy Vail *hadn't* been exaggerating this time.

Chapter 2

Longarm spent the next hour reading old newspaper articles concerning the gang's brutal activities during the past couple of years. When they robbed a stagecoach or an individual, they almost always shot a man's horse or one of his harness team, making escape impossible. After that, they rode up and ordered their victim to surrender his valuables—or his life. Only once had escape been possible, and that was by a muleskinner named George Jeffers who had leaped from the freight wagon into thick brush and managed to slip away from the thieves and eventually reach town. His had been a hollow victory, however, because he had been carrying the company's monthly payroll.

"Is Mr. Jeffers still in Flagstaff?" Longarm asked the editor. "Because, if he is, I'd like to have a word with him."

"Sure. He's employed by a local freighting outfit named Packers. They're located just down the street and have a big sign out in front. You can't miss it."

"What about the man who is offering a reward?" Longarm asked. "I'd like to speak to his wife."

"Oh no," the editor replied, wagging his head back and forth. "She has become very reclusive and refuses to even

14

think about the outrages she suffered, much less talk about them.''

"I'd like to speak to her anyway.''

"All right, but don't forget that you were warned. Her name is Mrs. Susan White and her husband is John White, a prominent politician and local businessman. He won't be happy if he learns that you have spoken to his wife concerning a matter that they both wish to forget.''

"I don't care if he's 'happy' or not. What's important is stopping this bunch. And besides, you said that the man was offering a sizable reward.''

"It's an *anonymous* reward, Marshal Long. I've advertised the reward, but no one knows for certain who is putting up the cash.''

"I see. All right, give me directions to her house.''

When he left the newspaper office, Longarm decided to interview George Jeffers first. He found the muleskinner harnessing a team. Longarm wasted no time and showed the man his badge. He then asked him to relate his harrowing experience with what most people were calling the Four Corners Gang.

"I wish I could tell you more than I told the editor,'' Jeffers began, "but it all happened so fast that I hardly had time to think about anything except getting out of there with my life.''

"I know,'' Longarm answered. "But there were a few details that I was hoping you might have skipped when you talked to Mr. Evans.''

"Such as?''

"What color horses were they riding?''

"Bays. All bays.''

Longarm was disappointed because bays were very common. "Did they have stocking feet? Blazed faces?''

"I don't remember.''

"Were the riders wearing masks?''

"Nope. That's why I figured they intended to kill me, so I made a run for it.''

"Good thinking, but, if they didn't wear masks, what did they look like?"

"I honestly can't say, Marshal. It was nearly sundown, and they wore hats pulled low over their faces. Two of them had long black hair which fell to their shoulders."

"Describe their clothing."

"They wore leather coats. Wool lined, I think."

"Were they armed with carbines or pistols?"

"Both. The one that shot my lead mule through the head used a Winchester. But the other two held pistols in their gloved fists. I know that because when I jumped and ran into the brush, they unleashed a swarm of bullets. I hit the dirt and crawled behind a big rock."

"So what happened next?"

"They came into the brush and tried to find and kill me. I never moved a muscle and was real scared. Finally, they gave up and I guess they figured I wasn't important enough to waste time on. I heard 'em whoppin' and carrying on while they counted out the company payroll."

"Is there anything else that you can think of that you might have forgotten or would be of value?"

"Nothing, except to say that they shoot first and ask questions later. Marshal, are you forming a posse?"

"I doubt it."

"It wouldn't help. No matter how many men you'd deputize, they'd get killed."

"What makes you so sure?" Longarm asked.

"Because the Four Corners Gang would lead you into an ambush, then empty saddles in a hurry. I've been thinking about them a lot since I was nearly killed, and I know I was real lucky."

"They can be tracked and captured or killed," Longarm said.

"Marshal, do you know how rough the country is up to the northeast past the Painted Desert into Four Corners?"

"No."

"I do. That's Black Mesa country. Lawless Navajo and

16

Hopi country. There ain't a hell of a lot of water, and what there is you got to hunt hard to find. There's quicksand along the Little Colorado, and everything up toward the Four Corners either bites, stings or will kill you on sight. The Navajo will steal your horse, then grin and watch you die of thirst. The Hopi once tossed a couple of Franciscan priests off their mesa tops, so they don't much care to be bothered, either."

"You make my chances sound pretty bad."

"They're worse than bad! Did the editor tell you how many bounty hunters have tried to track those killers?"

"Yes."

"Well, that ought to tell you a thing or two," Jeffers snapped. "Some of them were worthless and foolish to go off alone. But others were experienced hunters and trackers who knew their business. Didn't matter, though. They was killed same as the rest."

Longarm folded his arms across his chest. "You're trying to tell me something, so why don't you get to the point?"

"My point is that I don't believe they can be tracked down and killed as long as they're hiding in that badland Indian country up near the Four Corners. I have one more piece of bad news for you."

"I'm listening."

"There are probably more than three men in the gang. I heard a fella say that he saw five of them together, but he was riding a faster horse than they rode and got clean away."

This was indeed troubling news to Longarm, although not especially surprising.

"My bet," Jeffers continued, "is that there's a nest of 'em operating up around Four Corners and they probably have a hideout or stronghold. I'm guessing they fan out and raise hell in all directions. When they return, they share their bounty with the Navajos to keep quite and discourage anyone from entering their lands."

17

"That's quite a theory," Longarm drawled.

"Well, that's what I think, and I'm more often right about such things than I am wrong. But either way, they'll kill you and anyone you take into their territory."

"So the law is just supposed to let them continue to prey on innocent folks like yourself?"

"That's what the law has decided to do," Jeffers said, "and although folks in these parts are pretty disgusted with Marshal Potter, they think he's being smart."

Longarm had heard more than he wanted to hear and was pretty certain that Jeffers had no additional information, so he excused himself and went to see Mrs. Susan White.

She lived in an impressive Victorian mansion just a few blocks north of the train depot. When Longarm knocked on her door, the woman appeared, wearing black as though in mourning.

"What do you want?" she demanded.

Mrs. White was in her forties, a trim, attractive woman with graying hair and a stern expression. She was tall and statuesque with a rather superior bearing that Longarm usually associated with the wealthy and prominent people in smaller towns.

"Mrs. White, I'm Deputy Marshal Custis Long with the Denver Marshal's office. I've been asked to investigate the gang that has terrorized so many fine people, such as yourself."

"Go away!"

The woman started to leave, but Longarm got his toe in the door and pushed it open. Mrs. White turned and said in a hard, uncompromising tone of voice, "If you really are the law, you will know that you have just broken it by entering my home. Now, will this have to become very unpleasant or will you just leave right now?"

"I'm probably going out into the desert after those men," Longarm said, ignoring her question. "And I doubt that I'll have anyone with me."

"Then you are a fool."

"That may well be true, ma'am. But I am the law, and my boss has asked me to handle this business."

"Then he is also a fool. Ignore him. Quit your position if necessary, because if you go after that gang, you are a dead man."

"Ma'am, I've been tracking down and arresting outlaws for more years than I care to admit. I've hunted men from Montana to Arizona, and I've always come back alive and with my man . . . dead or alive."

"There are *three* men in this case. All of them blood-lusting and without morals or conscience. You won't have a chance."

"That's what Mr. Jeffers said over at Packers."

"Then you should have listened to him more carefully."

"I read the account of what happened. Your name was never mentioned."

"Shame on Mr. Evans for divulging it to you!"

"I *need* your help," Longarm said flatly. "Maybe you can tell me something that will give me an edge."

"No."

"All right then," Longarm said, backing out on the porch. "But you should know that you could have made the difference—in case I am killed."

That got her. Longarm saw the woman shake and then take a half step forward. "Come back inside," she whispered. "I will tell you what I can despite the pain it brings me."

"Thank you, Mrs. White."

She led him into a parlor, and Longarm sat on a velvet sofa across from a wall of books. Beautifully-framed pictures and awards decorated the other walls.

"Tea or coffee?" she asked.

"Neither, ma'am, because I won't be staying but a few minutes. I want to know if you could identify all or any of the three men who caught you out riding alone that afternoon and then abused and robbed you."

Her voice carried a tremor. "I can remember their faces. I shall *never, ever* be able to forget them."

"Then describe the men, one by one."

"They were as alike as curs weaned from the same mongrel litter. They were short and . . ."

"How short?"

"Five-eight or five-foot-nine. Not much taller than myself. But they were very powerfully built and very filthy."

"Features?"

"Jutting jaws, close-set black eyes. Thick lips. Long, dirty black hair."

"Do you think they were brothers?"

She nodded her head vigorously. "I'm almost sure they were related."

"Did they refer to each other by name?"

"No, but they laughed a good deal as they were . . . were using me."

"I'm sorry."

"Not half as sorry as I am."

"Is there anything else you can tell me?"

"Yes! Go back to Denver and grow old."

"I have to go after them, ma'am. If I don't, they'll keep it up and more people will be killed, robbed or abused." Longarm got up with his hat in his hand. "Thank you for your time, and I'm sorry for the pain I've just caused."

"Wait."

Longarm turned at the door and paused.

"They mentioned the Little Colorado and its canyons."

"I understand that there are also many mesas up in the Four Corners country."

"So I've heard," she replied. "I haven't been much help, have I?"

"More than you realize."

He was out on the porch now, and she had followed him outside. In better light, Custis saw that she was even more attractive than he'd first believed, though she carried a sadness in her eyes that went soul-deep. It occurred to him that

20

she might not be as old as she appeared and that the grayness in her hair might even be premature, caused by the horror of what she'd endured.

"Marshal Long?"

"Yes?"

"Why didn't they just kill me? I would have preferred a quick death."

Tears began to roll down her pale cheeks. "Mrs. White," he said gently, "they didn't kill you because they thought that you would suffer greatly of humiliation. They probably even thought you would somehow believe you were at fault."

"I *was!* Had I not been so stupid to go off riding alone. . . ."

Longarm instinctively reached for the woman, but she retreated, shaking her head. He took a deep breath and said, "Ma'am, if you continue to blame yourself, they will have accomplished exactly what they hoped. However, if you deny them that satisfaction, when I kill or arrest them, I will say that you never let them break your spirit."

She stared at him for a moment, and then a faint smile touched her pale lips. "Would you really do that for me?"

"I don't tell lies about important things, Mrs. White. And this is *very* important. Isn't it?"

"Yes. Very important."

Longarm smiled even though he didn't feel like it at the moment. "Then that's what I'll tell them."

"All right, Marshal Long. Starting today. Starting right this very minute, I will do everything I can to be strong."

"Good! You have no cause for guilt and need to live the rest of your life with courage and optimism."

"If you succeed in finding those three, I wouldn't object if you killed them."

"I'm no executioner, ma'am. The law doesn't work that way."

"A pity in this case. I'm far from being the only one that they've hurt badly."

"I know."

"Good luck." She came over and gave him a hug and then disappeared back inside her house. Longarm heard the woman lock her door. He sure hoped she would recover, but he wasn't too optimistic. Some people just always had to feel guilty about something.

He was marching back toward the lodge when Hilda breathlessly darted into his path. "Why, Custis, darling! Where have you been! I missed you."

She bumped her hip against his, but Mrs. White was strong on Custis's mind, so he said, "Hilda, we need to talk."

"I'd like that, but can't it wait until—"

"No," he told her, "it can't. I have a job to do, and I'm leaving."

Hilda's smile died. "You're leaving me?"

"Have you heard about the Four Corners Gang that is robbing and killing people?"

"You mean the ones that raped that woman and whose husband is putting up a five-hundred dollar reward?"

"The very same."

"Yeah, I heard about 'em. But, darling, everyone says that you're as good as dead if you go after them."

"I'm a federal deputy marshal, and it's my job."

Hilda blinked and took his hands. "Why don't we make love a while and then talk about this trouble? Maybe you could quit and find a job in Flagstaff. We could be together all the time then and—"

"No," he said gently. "I like my job, and besides, I'm not sure that I could satisfy you on a regular basis."

"Betcha could!" She winked, wiggled and giggled.

"Hilda, running down outlaws is my job, and it's the only thing I do really well."

"No it isn't," she told him, looking down at where his legs forked. "You do something else awfully well."

He blushed and looked around, relieved to see that no

one was near enough to have overheard her compliment. "Thanks."

"Could we just do it one last time before you leave?"

Longarm chuckled and took her arm. "Sure, Hilda," he replied, thinking about how everyone had warned him that he was as good as dead if he took up this outlaw trail. "I'd like that a lot," he said, as they cut across the lawn and headed for his room and what he knew would be a very vigorous bout of lovemaking.

Longarm just hoped it wouldn't be his last.

Chapter 3

Longarm wasn't a man to waste much time once he'd reached a decision. He went to the telegraph office and wired Billy Vail for enough money to buy a pair of quality saddle and pack horses as well as heavy bedrolls and all the other supplies he'd need for the long trail he was about to follow.

He ended his telegram to Billy by saying:

> *I don't much like the idea of going into the Four Corners alone after this gang and everyone thinks I'm a fool for trying, but I'd rather do it myself than get a bunch of gun-happy amateurs looking for glory and the posted reward money. I am going to cross into the Navajo and Hopi country and maybe I will find help among those people, but I don't count on it. If I fail to return, send the best men you have for this job, because this is a vicious, murdering gang of cutthroats and rapists that need to be captured, tried and then hanged.*

The livery man who sold Longarm the horses, saddles and packing supplies shook his head sorrowfully when Longarm was ready to leave Flagstaff. "Marshal Long," he said, "I sure admire your courage, but not your intelligence. Going after that bunch alone is certain suicide."

"Well," Longarm told the frowning man, "I've been counted out many a time and always seemed to find a way to survive."

"Maybe you were just lucky," the livery man observed as he spat a stream of chewing tobacco into the dirt. "They say a cat has nine lives, but even a cat gets killed sooner or later."

"Thanks for the encouraging words," Longarm offered dryly as he reined his horse around and started out of town.

"Custis!"

It was Hilda. Her rosy cheeks were streaked with tears. "If you live, will you come back to me?"

"I . . . I can't make any promises," he hedged. "I'm going to try to take the gang alive. That means I'll be needing to escort them to the nearest federal marshal's office. I don't even know yet where that might be."

"Oh, please come back!" she cried, following along beside his horse. "I will miss you so much."

"Find a good man to keep happy, and I'll kick him out of your bed if I return. Fair enough?"

She sniffled and managed a smile. "Good-bye, darling!"

"So long."

The last person Longarm talked to was Susan White. She was standing beside a porch pole in front of Hanson's Mercantile, and when he touched the brim of his hat in respect, she came out to say good-bye, carrying a package wrapped in linen.

"I didn't expect to see you again," he said.

"Nor did I expect to see you, Marshal. But I wanted to say how much your visit meant to me."

"I'm glad."

"You're a fine man, and I will grieve for you if things go bad."

"I'm tough to kill," he told her. "That's not bragging,

25

it's fact. You can ask a lot of men in federal prisons, and they'll tell you the same thing.''

"I see." She swallowed hard, looked up and said, "I wanted to give you something good to eat and also something for luck.''

"I could use both," he replied, taking the package. "And thanks.''

"Marshal Long?"

"Yes?"

"If I were single and a few years younger, I would do anything in my power to try to stop you from going after that bunch. But, having told you that, I hope you track those animals down and bring them to a swift, final justice.''

"I understand, Susan.''

"Do you, really?''

"Yes.'' Longarm impulsively reached down, and his fingers brushed her hair. "Don't worry," he said, "I'll get every last one of them, and they'll hang.''

She took a deep breath and then retreated to the boardwalk. Longarm could feel her eyes on his back until he rounded a corner and lined out for the Indian country, most everyone in Flagstaff writing him off as good as dead.

Longarm had never spent much time in the land of the Navajo and the Hopi, and he certainly had no idea of what to expect. He'd heard about this vast, arid land where the colors were as rich as a sunset and, frankly, he was eager to see the Hopi mesas and the great gorge of the Little Colorado River. He had four canteens and an extra keg of water for his horses and enough grub to last for two weeks. Longarm also carried a Winchester and plenty of ammunition for his double-action Colt revolver. He wore his Colt high on his left hip, butt tilted forward because he favored the cross draw. Longarm also carried an Ingersol railroad watch whose chain was soldered to a hide-out twin barrel .44 caliber derringer that had saved his bacon in more than one tight fix.

The first night out he dry camped in a shallow ravine and closely hobbled and tied both horses. Custis knew that the Navajo and probably the Hopi as well were experts who prided themselves at stealing a white man's horse. And to be stranded afoot out in this harsh, arid country would be a serious problem. Longarm did light a small fire, for there were clouds across the moon and he wished for at least a little light should he be jumped by enemies. As an extra precaution, he stuffed one of his bedrolls with brush so that it would appear to be inhabited, and then he took the other bedroll off a ways where he would actually sleep.

Susan White had baked him some chocolate cookies, and they were delicious. Longarm struggled to ration them out over the next few days and ate only four. He wished he had some coffee but decided to wait for that small pleasure until morning. When the fire began to sputter he went to his second bedroll and lay down on top of it with his boots on and his weapons close at his side. For about a half-hour he did nothing but listen to the night sounds, of which there were few. Just the sound of coyotes and once some kind of a bird scurrying through the brush. Satisfied that he was well hidden and unobserved, Longarm fell into a restful sleep and did not awaken until the sun peeped over the edge of his ravine. He rekindled his dead campfire, brewed coffee and fried salt pork. Ignoring the urge to devour Mrs. White's cookies, he instead selected several cold but nourishing sourdough biscuits and a can of peaches which he opened with his pocket knife. Before readying his horses, he gave them a hefty bait of oats and water from the keg. He could tell, however, that their thirst was not completely slaked.

"I hope to find a spring or a river by tonight," he told the horses. "But if not, we've got enough for at least another three days."

The horses nickered softly as if they understood. Longarm packed his gear, saddled his riding horse and was soon heading northeast again with the bright morning sun warming his cheeks. He could see big, billowing clouds off to the southeast and hoped that a storm might be heading his way. Desert storms could be sudden and intense, but they were rarely long in duration. Still, a man could often find the remains of these storms cradled in small rock basins, especially under the shadow of rocks and out of the hot sun. These little basins could provide a man and his animals with enough life-giving water to last for days until the next storm. That was how the Indians survived in this desert country when a lot of white men would perish.

That same afternoon Longarm stopped for a breather atop a high ridge and gazed back along the trail he'd climbed. That's when he saw a rider following him about two miles to the south. Longarm frowned and watched the horse and rider until they disappeared behind a hill. He waited another half hour for them to reappear, but they never did, so he figured the horseman did not want to be detected.

Friend or enemy?

There was a chance that someone friendly to the Four Corners Gang, or even one of the gang members, had gotten wind of his intentions and was hoping to surprise and ambush him. It was a chance that Longarm could not allow, so he led his horses into some rocks, drew out his Winchester and settled in for however long it took before the stranger reappeared.

It did not take long, and when the rider came into full view and rode past, Longarm stepped out from the rocks and shouted, "All right, reach for the sky!"

The rider did as he was ordered. Longarm moved around to get a better look at him and saw that it was, of all things, a woman! She was in her early twenties, slender and dressed like a man with a hat pulled down low and a bandanna wrapped around her neck. Most of her hair was tucked under her hat, but what he saw was light brown. She had nice features, but they were sunburned, bringing out a splash of freckles.

"Who the hell are you?"

"Can I put my arms down?" she asked.

"All right." Longarm lowered his rifle barrel. "But keep them in plain sight atop your saddle horn and answer my question."

"My name is Molly Murphy."

"What are you doing out here all alone, and why are you trailing me?"

She chewed her lower lip and gave him a frown. "It's a free country, ain't it, Marshal?"

"Of course it is, but that doesn't give you the right to stick to my back trail."

"Why not? You're just following someone else's old trail, ain't you?"

That was true, but it also seemed to Longarm to be irrelevant. "You don't belong out in this country," he said. "Haven't you heard of the Four Corners Gang?"

"Sure! They're the reason I'm following you."

"You want to have a run-in with them?"

"I want to shoot them dead and claim that five-hundred-dollar reward."

"Not a chance."

"Why not?" Molly leaned forward in the saddle. "What's the matter, do you want it all for yourself?"

"Don't be ridiculous. I'm a federal marshal, so I can't claim *any* of it," he told her with mounting exasperation.

"That's what Marshal Potter said, but I just wanted to make sure." She managed a thin smile. "It's good to have a clear understanding between us, don't you think?"

"I think that you are either addled by the sun or very foolish," Longarm replied. "Now turn that horse around and head on back to wherever it is you came from."

"I can't do that," she answered, jaw muscles cording and green eyes flashing with defiance. "You see, there's a reason why I have to find those outlaws and help you bring them to justice."

"Sure there is—you want the money."

29

"There's more to it than that. Way more," she told him.

"You may think you have a good reason, but you're wrong, Miss Murphy. I work alone, and I'm not about to have you for company."

Molly surveyed the dry, inhospitable badlands up ahead. "You may not know it yet, Marshal, but you need help. I know this country, but I understand you don't."

"How does a young lady like you know what it's like up in Indian and Four Corners country?"

"My father was a prospector, then an Indian agent. I know the Navajo, and without my help, you're liable to get your scalp lifted."

"I don't believe you."

"You're not very trusting, are you?"

"Nope."

"Then I'll tell you another reason why you need me."

"There's nothing you can say. I work alone. Always have."

"Without me, you'll die alone."

"I'll take my chances. Now go away!"

"Marshal, I know that I'm young and don't look like much, but don't let my looks fool you. I'm a crack shot. Want me to show you?"

"No," he told her. "Just turn that mare around and head south. I haven't got time to waste arguing."

"I talked to Potter, and he said that you didn't stand a chance of killing or capturing the gang alone. When I told him that I meant to come and help, he just laughed. Then I drew my six-gun and shot the picture of some varmint on a wanted poster dead center through his eye. I did it so fast that the laughter died in his stupid throat, and he didn't have any more words to say."

"You fired a gun in Marshal Potter's office?"

"I did. And then, just to show that worthless dog that I hadn't gotten lucky, I shot the varmint's *other* eye out!" Molly beamed, looking very proud of herself.

"Miss Murphy, even if you were Annie Oakley herself,

I couldn't allow you to come along with me. It's just too dangerous.''

"Don't you think I got a right to decide about my own life?"

"Exactly how old *are* you?"

"I'm old enough to do what I shouldn't, but wise enough to know better."

"That doesn't answer my question."

"All right," she said, "I'm twenty-two."

"No!"

"Okay then, twenty, and that is the gospel truth."

Longarm sighed. He supposed it was the truth, but twenty was still mostly a girl. Molly, however, had a stubborn streak, and it was one that he needed to nip in the bud right this minute.

"I'm ordering you to head on back to town."

"I won't do it!"

He took several threatening steps toward the girl, but she didn't move and said, "Marshal Long, you can't stop me from riding north."

Longarm choked the stock of his rifle in frustration and then whirled around and stomped back into the rocks. He shoved his Winchester in its saddle boot, gathered his lead rope and mounted. When he rode out, Molly Murphy hadn't moved a muscle.

"Go away! This is no country for a crazy young woman."

"I *owe* the gang, Marshal!"

"What does that mean?"

Her voice went dead, and he had to lean forward in the saddle to hear her whisper, "They killed my father and . . . violated my mother and me less than two years ago."

"Where?"

"Just to the north. We were prospecting when they caught us."

"I'm sorry," he said, thinking of Mrs. White and hoping this girl wasn't as badly scarred.

31

"I ain't looking for pity, Marshal."

"You want revenge," he said.

"That's right."

"Go home. Take care of your mother or do whatever it is you do."

"What I do," she grated, "is dream of the moment when I can kill them! All I've been doing these past few years is preparing for the day when I'd go after them and settle the score."

Longarm reined his horse up short. "Look, Molly. I am sorry about what these men did, and I've learned enough about them to know that they neither ask nor give any quarter. It would be bad enough if they kill me but even worse if they got their hands on you a second time. You understand that, don't you?"

She nodded and swallowed hard. It took quite an effort for her to say, "Oh, I understand what you're saying, Marshal. And I appreciate the fix I'm putting you in right now, but I'll repay you with your life."

"Talk is cheap, Molly. I can't take the responsibility for you."

"Then don't!" she snapped in anger. "But I'm not turning back no matter what you say."

"I could arrest you for obstructing justice."

She laughed, and it was not a pretty sound. "What possible good would that do? You gonna handcuff me or take me all the way back to Flagstaff? If you did that, Potter would turn me loose in a day or two because I'd badger him half to death and then I'd come right back here and follow your trail north."

Longarm knew he was losing the argument but said, "What if I shot that mare out from under you? Then, you'd have to walk back to town."

She blanched. "You wouldn't!"

Longarm ran a bluff. He unholstered his gun, cocked back the hammer and aimed it at the mare's head. It was a pretty buckskin with long, clean legs and a deep chest. All

32

in all, the mare was a fine animal, but he took aim anyway, hoping that the woman would lose her nerve.

"If you kill my horse, I'll follow on foot," she breathed, looking scared but resolute. "I won't turn back, but I might just steal one of your horses some night. How do you do without sleep?"

"Not well," he admitted.

"Then put the gun away and let's stop this nonsense and talk about how we are going to find this gang."

Longarm holstered the Colt, trying hard to figure out some way to discourage this woman before she became a complete nuisance. "Molly, be reasonable! I'm a federal marshal, and this is what I'm hired to do."

"And it's what I *have* to do!"

Longarm ground his teeth and said, "You don't have much water in those two canteens. Not nearly enough to travel this country."

"I didn't have the money to buy no keg to haul it in nor a pack animal to carry it, but my father knew where to find the waterholes, and I recollect a few. I'll be all right. In fact, I'll probably save your bacon when that keg runs dry and your mouth tastes like desert sand."

"That's debatable. I have plenty of water and you don't. So turn around and git while your horse is still able."

Her eyes reached past him. "That gang doesn't carry but a couple extra canteens, so there have to be springs and the like around here someplace. All we got to do is to follow their tracks to water when we run dry."

"You think it is that simple, huh?"

"It is that simple unless you insist on complicating things," she told him. "The fact is that I can't be chased or scared off, and I'm coming with you."

Longarm muttered and then he fumbled for a cigar. He smoked for a few moments, trying to decide if there was any possible solution to this new complication. He finally decided there was not, so he rode on without a word and didn't look back all the rest of that morning. About midafternoon, he stopped again and this time watered his horses from the keg, making a big show of how much they needed and appreciated the water and how sorrowful it was that Molly's poor mare had to suffer of thirst. Now and then, he glanced over at the girl and could see that she was deeply troubled. Maybe, he hoped, she would soon become discouraged and turn back. He could also see that her mare was suffering from lack of water and hardly sweating a drop.

They rode on through the rest of the warm afternoon, and once he twisted around in the saddle to see the woman giving her mare water from her canteen. She was trying to do it with cupped hands. The buckskin was sucking it up like crazy, but a lot was spilled. Longarm felt guilty as sin, but this was no time to go weak and change his stance. If she came along, chances were that she would get killed and probably also get him killed.

With sunset he made a second day's dry camp and measured his own water supply, disturbed by how fast it was shrinking. He wondered if she really did know the location of a few local waterholes and decided she must not or she would have gone off to give her horse a drink by now.

Longarm built a campfire on low ground and hobbled his horses after giving them more of his precious water and grain. When he peered back into the gathering dusk, he saw that she was gone.

Good riddance. She finally saw the sense in going back to wherever it was she came from and letting a lawman do a lawman's job.

Longarm bedded down a ways from his fire after making his dummy sleeper and looked up at the stars. He thought about Molly Murphy and sure hoped her mare was strong enough to reach water before it collapsed and died of thirst. And what if it was not? Should he go back just to make sure she made it out safe? He fretted about that until nearly midnight and decided that Molly was too smart to die out here and would find a way to reach Flagstaff. She'd be angry and maybe even bitter that he'd denied her a share of his water keg and forced her to go back, but he'd done it for her own good and it had certainly not given him any sense of victory or pleasure.

"Molly, I'll do my best for you and Mrs. White and all the others that have suffered because of this bunch," he vowed to the stars above. "I swear that I will."

With that, Longarm closed his eyes and finally went to sleep. He was in Navajo country now and would have to watch his horses very carefully or they would be stolen the first minute he became lax or careless.

But he wouldn't let down his guard and maybe he'd have some luck tomorrow and find water. He sure needed to, the way the water in his keg was dropping.

Chapter 4

Longarm awoke early and was back in the saddle gnawing on a cold biscuit soon after sunrise. He knew that his horses were thirsty again but didn't dare give them water until he had some hope of replenishing his supply. Longarm gazed up at the rising sun and figured today would be even hotter than yesterday. Licking his cracked lips, he vowed that he would not drink until thirst became a torment. He gazed hopefully to the sky, but the dark thunderclouds that he had seen a few days earlier were absent, and there was no hope of rain.

"We'll find water," he vowed, taking up the clear outlaw trail that he'd been following. "It can't be far up ahead."

But he was wrong. The morning passed with the temperature soaring into the nineties. Longarm became so dry that he could barely swallow, and he knew that his animals were suffering.

Could I have been so wrong that I'm riding into a death trap without a shot being fired?

This was the question Longarm kept asking himself as the blistering morning slowly wore past. He stopped at noon and rationed water to his horses and then a few sips for himself. Longarm knew the best thing he could do was

36

to find some shade and hole up for the afternoon and then travel at night, but the trail he followed often passed over hard rock, and it would be nearly impossible to follow in the dark. He kept moving.

It was nearly sundown when Longarm crawled up a red-rocked hillside and dismounted to stare out at the endless emptiness of barren rocks and sun-suffering trees and sage. Had he not been so thirsty and discouraged, Longarm might have appreciated the incredible and varied rainbow colors of the Painted Desert. Beautiful at any time, it was never more magnificent than at sunrise and sunset. As far as he could see were broken buttes, towering stone spires jutting into the pastels of a sunset sky.

But where could he ever find water?

In vain, Longarm's eyes searched for a stand of cotton-woods or vivid greenery that would betray the presence of life-saving water. He saw nothing but rock and sage and the stunted juniper and pinion pines that were common in this high desert country.

Longarm expelled a deep breath and then climbed out of his saddle to stand, swaying with fatigue. He would have to discover water tomorrow because his keg was nearly empty, and it was far too late to turn back now.

With that thought in mind, Longarm made another dry camp and fell into an exhausted sleep after giving his animals and himself only a token measure to drink and eat.

He awoke before dawn with the feeling that he was not alone. Longarm drew his gun and gazed down toward his horses and the remains of last night's campfire. Sure enough, someone was there rifling through his camp.

Longarm eased himself erect and swallowed hard and then moved forward. When he was sure that he had the intruder in pistol range, he said, "Freeze! One move and I'll drill a hole in you big enough for a crow to fly through!"

"So," Molly Murphy said, dropping Longarm's dummy

bedroll and shaking her head, "you'd actually shoot me just for stealing a few lousy biscuits?"

"Dammit! I told you to go back!"

"I know, but instead I'm here to save your skin, just like I promised," she told him, munching loudly on a biscuit. "So why don't you come over here and have something to eat and stop being so grouchy?"

"You fool!" he raged with exasperation. "Don't you know that we're almost out of water!"

"*You* might be, but I'm not."

His jaw sagged. "You found water!"

"Sure did. Not a mile from here, and I'm a little disappointed that you didn't see it, too."

He took a deep breath. "You're not lying to me, are you?"

"Of course not!" She shoved a canteen toward him. "It's full and sweet, so drink as much as you like because there is plenty more where that came from."

Longarm didn't need any urging.

"If your horses are as thirsty as they look, why don't you saddle up and follow me over to the spring where they can drink their fill."

"I'll do that," Longarm said. "And . . . well, thank you."

"If you capture and get the Four Corners Gang on a gallows, that's all the thanks that I'll be wanting."

"Like I said before, I'll do my best."

"How good *is* your best?"

"It's pretty good," he said.

"I'll bet you're not as handy with a gun as I am," she boasted.

Longarm ignored the thinly veiled challenge and saddled his horse and then got his pack animal lined out. "Molly," he said, "let's go have a long drink and then an even longer talk."

"There's not a lot to talk about, Marshal. The bald truth of this situation is that you can talk until you're blue in the face, but I'm not turning back. You can't make me, and besides, you need me.''

''For what?''

''For what!'' Molly placed her hands on her shapely hips and laughed. ''For keeping you and your horses alive! Don't you know that there is no more water for more than twenty hard miles!''

''I'd have made it,'' he grumbled.

''In a sow's dirty ear you would have! Marshal, you'd have missed it, just like you missed the one we're about to enjoy right now.''

Longarm wasn't in the habit of being spoken to like that by anyone, much less a smart aleck young woman. But he could not ignore the truth of Molly's uncompromising words. He was not a good desert traveler—never had been or would be. Longarm much preferred the cooler country and the high mountains of Montana, Wyoming and Colorado. Out here when a man got dry and hot, he couldn't even think properly.

''Follow me,'' Molly said much too cheerfully. ''Your salvation is at hand!''

She led him across a mile of desert and then around a rock-strewn hillock, and there was the spring, complete with cottonwoods and even an acre of grass for the horses. It was an oasis in the desert with the charred and littered remains of hundreds of old campfires. Longarm turned his horses loose, knowing that they would never leave until he made them do so. Dropping fully stretched on the side of a pond, Longarm drank his fill and then ducked his head in the water and closed his eyes with a sigh of pure contentment.

When he finally recovered, he walked over to Molly, who was sitting in the shade of a tree, grinning. ''Are you a believer yet, or do you want to test the wilderness and go through hell again?''

''I have writing materials in my saddlebags,'' he said in

a flat voice, "so why don't you just tell me where to find the next waterhole?"

"Nope! Not a chance." She cocked her head slightly to one side and regarded him with what he believed to be something far short of admiration. "You sure are a stubborn fool."

"Stubbornness is not always bad," he countered. "It's actually a trait that has saved my life and got me my man a good many times. And Molly, the one thing I can't abide besides a man that mistreats a woman or an animal, is a quitter."

"Well, you're no quitter, that's for sure. But neither am I, Marshal. So, the way that I see things, we might as well shake hands and join company."

"I'm supposed to give in?"

"Yep." Molly looked north, and her brow furrowed. "We're going after a pack of thieves, rapists and killers who have every advantage except surprise. And even that would have been lost if you'd have stumbled around in this country much longer."

"You don't mince words, do you?"

"I sure don't," she told him. "And I don't make idle brag."

"Neither do I."

"Let me show you how good I am with a gun," she said, standing and looking off to find a challenging target. "There! See that white quartz rock sitting on top of that big boulder?"

"Sure."

"Watch!"

Molly's hand covered her gun butt, and the gun flashed downward. Her Colt lifted and fired in one smooth motion so suddenly that it was the mere blink of an eye. Longarm had been watching her hand, but when he looked up, the quartz rock was missing.

"I could do it again if you don't believe what you saw

just now," she offered with her usual cockiness. "It wasn't luck."

"I believe you, Molly."

"Why don't you show me what *you* can do just so we understand each other."

"No thanks."

"What!"

"I don't draw unless I mean to kill something," he told her.

"You're just saying that because you can't outdraw or outshoot me!"

"That might be true and it might not be true," he conceded, "but I'm not going to make this a shooting contest. Are you as good with a rifle?"

"I told you that I was."

"Get mine, and let's see."

Molly went to his horse and then changed her mind and marched over to her own animal saying, "I prefer to fire my own weapon."

She drew a double-barreled shotgun from her saddle scabbard and smiled. "It's the best shotgun money can buy, and it cost my father forty-six dollars."

"It's worthless out here," Longarm said with disgust. "What's the matter, can't you fire a rifle?"

"Sure! But I like the shotgun better."

"Suit yourself," Longarm told her, wondering if she really could fire a rifle with any accuracy.

Well, he thought, *it appears that I have damn little choice but to wait and suddenly find out.*

"What is your plan?" Molly asked a short while later as they waited out the midday heat and let their horses graze.

"My plan is to hunt them down and capture them alive."

She snorted with disgust. "*That's* a plan?"

"It's my plan," he said. "And it usually works."

"Well, it damn sure won't this time!"

"You got a better one?"

"No," she admitted. "Not yet, at least."

"Then we use my plan until you come up with something better."

"So that's it, huh?" she asked, looking at him closely.

"Yep."

Longarm closed his eyes and pulled his hat over his face. "I'm going to take a nap while the horses graze. I suggest that you do the same, because if we can follow the tracks, I plan on riding all night."

"We don't need to follow the tracks. I know this bunch. They're heading for wherever they hole up between their southern raids. Pa guessed that would be somewhere to the east of the mesas."

"The Hopi mesas?"

"What else? Marshal, don't you know *anything* about this country and what there is up near Four Corners?"

"Of course I do," he bluffed. "But I just wanted to know what *you* know."

"Well, I obviously know a lot more than you do. Anyway, we ought to angle more to the east and hope we don't run into the Navajo."

"And if we do?"

"Then we'll have to present them with gifts and trust that they're not interested in killing us and taking our horses. But the Navajo generally don't want a fight. They'd far rather rob you blind."

"I'm going to take a nap and give this some thinking," he decided aloud. "You ought to do the same."

"Can I trust you with my eyes closed?"

Longarm scowled. "What is that supposed to mean?"

"It means that you're a man and I'm a woman and we are a long ways from a preacher or our mothers," Molly blurted. "So let's understand one thing right now—I'm not interested in anything you have to offer except your pledge to kill or capture this gang. Is that understood?"

"Yes, and I feel the same way. The last thing I need is a romp on the rocks. I'm all business."

She snorted. "I somehow doubt that."

Longarm had had his fill of her sassiness. "Wake me up at sundown."

He awoke at sundown. When Longarm sat up and rubbed his eyes, he saw Molly down by the horses. She was bent over cleaning her buckskin mare's feet, checking them for stone bruises and cracks, which was something Longarm figured he also ought to be doing. He paused for a few minutes to regard her pretty buttocks, so tight now in her Levi's, and the perfect curve of her hips and long, shapely legs. Longarm had not taken the time to appreciate Molly's womanly appearance, but he knew he didn't need that kind of distraction, so he climbed to his feet and started forward to join her.

"Hi," he said, coming down to check out the hooves of his animals. "Did you take a nap?"

"Of course not!"

"Why?"

"I just didn't figure that, given as how loud you snore, I could take the chance."

"I *didn't* snore!" he protested with indignation.

"Sure, and skunks don't stink." Molly finished her inspection and said, "I think we ought to get moving."

"I was thinking the same, but we need to take time to eat. I've got salt pork and more biscuits in my pack."

"I know. I already ate a bunch."

"You sure know how to help yourself to someone else's vittles," he grumbled.

"I'm not bashful or in the habit of going hungry," Molly replied, tightening her cinch and then bridling the buckskin.

Longarm prepared to leave, but not before refilling his water keg and canteens. As they were riding out, he cast a baleful eye back at the spring and hoped that Molly was right and that they would find another just like it after twenty miles. If that was true, they would be there by morning, and the horses would get another chance to graze on spring-fed grass and regain more strength and stamina.

"Marshal Long?" she asked around midnight.

"Yeah?"

"Did you *really* tell that poor fella that manages the Big Elk Lodge that a *bear* tried to use that broken hammock?"

"How'd you know—"

"I know a lot more than you might think," she interrupted. "Hilda and I are friends. She's the one that put me on to you."

"Hilda sent you after me?"

"Well, not exactly. But she told me all about you, and that's why I don't trust you to be honorable with a poor, helpless, young woman."

He almost choked. "You may be young and poor, but you are anything but helpless, Molly."

"Well, yeah, that's true. I know that and so does Hilda, but I wanted to make sure that you knew it, too."

"And so that's why you wanted to have a shooting contest?"

"That, and to see if you're any good with something besides your trophy-sized pecker. Hilda says that you are hung like a stallion."

Longarm was glad it was dark, because he could feel his cheeks burn with embarrassment. Somehow, he managed a laugh.

"What's so damned funny!"

"You and Hilda," he replied. "And, if we weren't on a manhunt, I might even teach you a thing or two."

"If you did, I'd shoot your trophy pecker plumb off and send Hilda into deep mourning."

Longarm hooted with laughter, and then so did Molly.

Maybe, he thought, *every cloud does have a silver lining.*

Chapter 5

The next afternoon they saw a flock of buzzards swarming and circling over a pile of rocks.

"Could be a mustang," Molly said.

"Could be a man," Longarm replied. "We'd better ride over and find out."

They exchanged solemn glances before Longarm drew his rifle and took the lead. As they approached the red-necked and -headed turkey vultures, their horses grew agitated and snorted with fear.

"It's no horse," Longarm said, "it's a man."

The body was stretched out atop a slab of red rock. The vultures were tearing at it and making hissing noises as they fought for the remains.

"Shoot them!" Molly cried in horror.

But Longarm shook his head. "No, I don't want to risk someone hearing the shot. We might be closer to the outlaws than we think."

"Well, we have to do *something!*"

"I know. I won't just leave him lying there," Longarm answered, dismounting while still some distance from the remains. "Hold my reins and ride off downwind. It won't take long to cover the body with rocks."

Molly nodded and hurried off while Longarm made his

way to the remains. The stench of death made him want to gag. The corpse had been so ravaged by the vultures and other scavengers that it had no remaining facial features. Holding his breath and swearing at the hissing and swarming vultures who stayed just of out reach, Longarm grabbed the man by the ankles and dragged him off the rock. Fortunately, there was a cleft between two boulders that would serve as a tomb, and Longarm rolled the decomposing body down into the narrow space.

"I expect that you didn't die of an accident," he said, checking the corpse's pockets looking for identification. He found a letter and stuffed it into his pocket before he quickly covered the body with loose gravel, topping it with large rocks. Longarm worked fast, and the gruesome job was completed in only a few minutes.

Satisfied that the remains would be protected in a final resting place, he hurried back to Molly and their horses. The buzzards descended on the place where the decomposing body had rested, squawking and hissing. A few landed on the corpse's new resting place and danced around in flapping protest.

"I'd love to use them for target practice," a white-faced Molly vowed. "I'll bet I could kill six with six shots."

"Don't waste your ammunition," he told her. "And try to put the thought out of your mind."

"Easier said than done. You surprised me."

"Why?"

"Because you could have refused to take care of the body, but you didn't. That tells me that you are sensitive."

"Is that a compliment, or should I take it as a weakness?"

"A compliment. Burying that man wasn't easy, but it was right. And I'm ashamed to say I couldn't have mustered up the will to do it."

"He had a letter, but no wallet or anything of value on his person," Longarm said, retrieving the letter from his pocket and taking a close look at the name on the envelope.

46

"It's addressed to a Mike Hopewell, care of general delivery in Flagstaff."

"Oh, no!"

Longarm looked up quickly and saw that Molly's fingers were pressed to her lips and her face was ashen. He was about to open the letter and read it aloud, but now he paused. "Are you all right?"

"No," she whispered, "Mike Hopewell was a friend of mine. His father and my father were long-time prospecting partners, and we often came out to this country searching for gold or silver. Mike wanted to marry me when I was sixteen, but I wasn't interested, so he married someone else—but it didn't last."

"What do you suppose he was doing way out here?"

"I have no idea. Mike and I last talked about six months ago. He said that he hated his job and was going to make a big change."

Longarm was confused. "Are you saying that you think he became a member of the Four Corners Gang?"

"No chance of that," Molly said, shaking her head back and forth. "He hated them because of what they'd done not only to me and my father but also to other people he knew. Mike was trying to learn how to use a gun, and when he saw how good I'd become, it made him angry."

"Why?"

"He said that it was ridiculous for a woman to become an expert shot and think of revenge. I got mad at him, and we had a big fight."

Molly's expression was bleak, and Longarm saw tears glisten in her eyes as she continued. "I never saw him after that, but I heard Mike was drinking pretty hard and bragging that he was going to track down the gang and kill some of them for the reward."

"Well," Longarm told her, "I guess he tried."

"Damn them!" Molly whispered.

Longarm handed the letter to Molly. "You read it when you feel better. I doubt there is anything in that letter that

47

will help us get to the bottom of who killed Mike or why, but let me know if I'm wrong.''

Molly folded the letter and slipped it into her shirt pocket. "Let's ride," she said, studying the vultures. "We need to find the next waterhole, and I have a feeling that we are getting close to danger.''

Longarm studied her. "Any particular reason why you think that?''

"No, it's just a woman's intuition. I . . . I don't want to talk anymore for a while. All right?''

"Sure. Find water and we'll drink and rest in silence.''

"Good.''

Molly located the springs, although you'd have had to be blind to miss it since there were so many hoof prints in the vicinity. They all converged on the spring, which bubbled out of a low basin and was surrounded by bones, the ashes of old campfires, trees and grass. The spring had formed a pond whose surface was covered with floating moss and scum.

"This water will make you sick to your stomach if it isn't boiled,'' Molly warned.

"But it's okay for our horses?''

"Yes, they'll be fine. But I drank it once, and my stomach didn't forgive me for a week.'' Molly made a face. "I got the scoots, and it was awful!''

"Say no more,'' he told her. "I've a pan in my pack. We'll boil enough to replenish our keg and canteens. How much farther north before we run into someone?''

"I don't know,'' Molly admitted. "My father and I never prospected any farther north. Too dangerous.''

She pointed toward some distant buttes. "Those are the three Hopi mesas. I expect to run into them or at least come across their corn fields pretty soon.''

"They raise corn way up here in this high desert country?''

"That's what I've been told.''

"How do they irrigate it?" Longarm asked. "Is there a river or lake around someplace?"

"Nope. They raise corn, squash and beans on the scant rainfall this country receives. I'm told that their corn is colored red, yellow and even black. It's supposed to taste good."

"Do the Navajo also farm?"

"My pa said they aren't interested in farming but prefer to raise livestock."

"I wonder," Longarm mused, "if we'll meet any of them."

"I'd bet on it," Molly vowed. "The real question is, are they in the business of protecting the Four Corners Gang and will they try to stop or kill us?"

Longarm nodded with understanding. And although he would not have admitted it out loud, he was beginning to appreciate Molly Murphy. In most instances, his badge alone would ensure that he had some assistance in running down and capturing outlaws, but not in Indian country. Longarm had no illusions whatsoever that the Navajo or the Hopi would give a tinker's damn about a tin star.

After watering, unsaddling and hobbling their animals, they built a small fire of dry twigs which gave off very little smoke and settled in for the night. Longarm had no appetite and neither did Molly, but they forced down the remainder of their biscuits and a few bits of salt pork. Sundown came and then the sky filled with stars as they sat opposite the campfire, each lost in their own thoughts.

Finally, Molly said, "You're a federal marshal, and I suspect that you've been hunting down outlaws and murderers for a good long while."

"That's right."

"And so you've seen a lot of dead bodies, huh?"

"Listen, I've seen more than my share of death, but it's always a shock. And what we saw today, well, it would make anyone sick to their stomach."

"Yeah," she mused, eyes locked on the flames, "and I

49

can't help but wonder how my life and Mike's life would have gone had we married. If we had, maybe I wouldn't be out here now and he'd still be alive. Maybe we'd have a family and a little place in Flagstaff and be happier than—''

''Molly, stop it,'' Longarm ordered. ''If we start maybeing this and maybeing that whenever we come across sickness, ruination or death, we can drive ourselves crazy with guilt.''

She looked up. ''But I can't help thinking I should have married him.''

''Were you in love with Mike?''

''No, but—''

''Then you did the right thing not to marry,'' Longarm said. ''So stop kicking yourself for something that you had nothing to do about.''

''All right,'' she whispered, ''but, if I could turn back time, I'd have married him anyway and he'd still be alive.''

''Try to go to sleep.''

''What about you?''

Longarm lit a cigar from the embers of their campfire. ''I'll sit up and look over things for a while longer.''

''Then so will I.''

''No, if you can't sleep, then I'll do it now and you can try later.''

''I'll go to sleep,'' Molly promised as she stretched out on Longarm's extra bedroll. ''And I'll try to put Mike out of my mind.''

''Maybe you should give me that letter back.''

''No, I want to read it first.''

''Okay, but not tonight. Go to sleep, Molly Murphy.''

''If I get killed, you wouldn't let my—''

''Molly, stop it!'' he hissed.

''I will,'' she promised. ''I'll just blank the sight of poor Mike lying there as the vultures swarmed over him and think of something good.''

Longarm didn't believe her for one minute. He was back to the point where he wished she'd never come along because the young woman was very likely to see a good deal more death before they returned to Flagstaff—if they were lucky enough to return.

"Were you ever married?" she asked, rolling over and propping her head on a bent elbow.

"No."

"Why not? Didn't you ever find the right woman, or are you planning to marry our friend Hilda?"

"Shut up," he said without anger.

"You ought to quit this line of work when we've captured the Four Corners Gang and then go into something safe and respectable."

"I think being a federal deputy marshal is plenty respectable."

"Okay, but we both agree it's not safe."

"Being 'safe' bores me," he said. "I've been offered promotions like my boss Billy Vail's job, but that would mean a desk job, and I'd go crazy shuffling papers and looking out the window."

"You're hopeless," Molly told him.

"And you're not?"

She smiled. "We are a pair, all right. So what about Hilda?"

He smoked quietly for a few moments and then said, "Hilda thinks she is in love with every man who has the ability to take her to bed at least three times a day and then another couple of times a night. She probably found my replacement before I'd ridden five miles out of town.

"I like Hilda!" Molly said defensively.

"So did I! But I wasn't in love with her and I've no intention of getting married."

"Maybe you just haven't found the right woman."

"Go to sleep!"

"You aren't much of a talker when you have things on your mind that need discussing, are you?"

Longarm stood up and scratched. Then, with his cigar clenched between his teeth, he grated, "I think I'm going

51

to hike up to that big rock and take a look around. On a clear night like this, I'll bet I could see a campfire if it was fifty miles away."

"Don't break your leg in the dark," she warned. "I wouldn't want to have to put you out of your misery."

"Fat chance!"

"Marshal?"

He had been about to leave. "Yeah?"

"What's your first name?"

"Why?"

"Just tell me."

"All right, it's Custis."

"Custis. Well," she said, yawning, "I'm glad it isn't Custer."

Longarm shook his head and left their camp. He hiked up to a high jumble of rocks that he'd been studying all evening, and there was enough moon and starlight to make the task safe and easy. Then he sat down and surveyed the vast ocean of shadows and light until his eyes locked on a glowing spark far, far to the north. At least twenty miles, maybe thirty.

A campfire! Indian or outlaw? Rapist and killers or peaceful Hopi farmers protecting their precious corn fields? Navajo? No use worrying about it tonight. We'll find out soon enough.

He sat up until nearly midnight and then returned to his bedroll. Molly was sound asleep, and he did not awaken her. Longarm hoped that Molly was having sweet dreams but doubted she was, given the earlier sight of the vultures and poor Mike's corpse.

Chapter 6

"Wake up, sleepyhead," Molly said as she knelt beside Longarm. "The sun is well off the horizon, and it's time that we get on the move."

Longarm knuckled the sleep from his eyes. "You got the coffee boiling yet?"

"I sure do."

"Good," he said, climbing to his hands and knees and yawning. "You look rested."

"I wish that I could say the same about you."

"I was up late," he told her. "I spotted a campfire about a day's ride north."

"Do you think it's the Four Corners Gang?"

"I don't know, but we ought to find out tonight unless they're moving away from us."

Molly's brows knitted with concern, causing Longarm to say, "You've been a great help so far, but it's not too late for you to turn around and go home. In fact, I wish that you would."

"And leave you to face the gang alone? Not a chance!"

"It's my *job*," he told her. "It's what I get paid to do."

"I don't think you get paid enough to ride alone into this country after an entire gang!"

53

"Well, that's not the issue here," he replied. "I'm committed to capturing or killing this bunch, and there's nothing more to be said on the matter."

"We need help," Molly told him. "And not just a little help, but a bunch."

"Well," Longarm told her, reaching for the coffee pot, "help isn't coming, at least none that I know about. So don't even think about it."

In reply, Molly turned, snatched up her gun and emptied it into one of the rusty tin cans that was scattered around an old campfire. The can jumped three times, but then she missed twice before drilling it with the sixth shot.

"I'm usually more accurate, Custis."

"That's fine shooting by any measure," Longarm told her. "No need to apologize for the way you handle a gun. You keep six beans in the can, huh?"

"Yes. When we catch up with the gang, we're going to need every last bullet we can muster."

"I suppose that's true."

Molly turned to go get her buckskin saddled, but not before she asked, "So tonight we'll find out who made that campfire?"

"I expect so."

"Good," she replied. "Seeing what they did to Mike Hopewell makes me all the more determined."

"Have you read his letter?"

"Not yet."

"Maybe you should."

Molly reached into her pocket, unfolded the letter and then began to read:

Dear Mike,

> *I am sorry that things have not turned out well for you, but I sure hope you don't go after the Four Corners Gang for the reward and get yourself killed. I am living in Cortez, Colorado. Our son . . .*

54

Molly looked up with surprise. "Custis, I never knew they had a child together."

"Well, it happens. Read on and then maybe we can get some idea of what he thought he could do out here alone."

Molly took a deep breath and continued reading the letter.

. . . Our son is three years old now and very happy and healthy. Little Mike looks like you, but he seems to have a lot more sense. I know you worry about my new husband and how he treats Little Mike, but you have no need to fret because everything is good between the three of us. Bob's saddle repair business is doing real well and we live in a nice house we just bought. Everyone here is happy but I am real worried about this Four Corners Gang. I have heard of Yancy Hooker, the one that you say is the leader of the gang. His family hails from Cortez and they are hated and feared in this country. Sometimes they come to town and then everyone that can bolts their doors and closes up shop.

Molly looked up. "Did you know they were the Hookers?"

"No," Custis replied. "But we do now. Go on and finish the letter. Maybe there is more that we can learn about them."

Molly returned to reading.

Yancy and his brothers killed another family two years back. They were neighbors and feuding. I guess it was an awful slaughter and lots of people died. They also ran off our town marshal and so the Hookers pretty much do as they please. Fortunately, they are gone a lot and the rumor is that they have another big ranch down in northeastern Arizona, not

more than a hundred miles from here. I am also
happy to say that they like Bob and buy his saddles
and tack, paying a fair price. He even has two sad-
dles of theirs to repair right now! But I wish God
would come down and kill the lot of them cause we
don't need their blood money, or at least that's my
opinion. Anyway, if you come to Cortez wanting to
see Little Mike, that's okay by me but don't you dare
cause no trouble by trying to collect that reward on
the Hooker brothers. You'd only get yourself killed
and maybe us too, and I'd never forgive you for that.

                                        Sincerely,
                                        Dorothy.

"That was some letter," Longarm said. "But while it
tells us that Yancy Hooker is the leader, it doesn't offer
enough proof for me to make an arrest."

"Well," Molly said, "you can make up your own opinion, but I know what needs to be done, and I won't hesitate
to do it!"

Longarm took three swift steps forward, grabbed Molly
by both arms and lifted her right up on the tips of her toes.
"Now listen," he growled, "it's time we got something
settled right now. I'm in charge, and you'll do what I say!
Is that understood?"

She struggled, but he held her helpless in a viselike grip.
"Let go of me!"

"Not until you agree to follow my orders."

"And what if I refuse?"

"Then I'll take your mare and leave you right here to
wait for my return or, if I go down, someone else's. Is that
clear?"

"You wouldn't!"

"Try me," Longarm challenged. "I'm tired of you
threatening to open fire on the gang the minute we get them
in our gunsights."

"What else can we do?"

"I don't know, but I'll figure out something when the time comes. The important thing is that I am a United States deputy marshal and you *will* follow my orders. Is that clearly understood?"

"Yes, dammit!"

Longarm didn't release her yet but said, "I want your word on it."

"You have my word of honor!" Molly's eyes were blazing with anger. "Is this over now?"

"It is as long as you keep your word," he replied, turning her loose.

"You really make me mad!"

"Too bad, Molly. But I'm not here to impress or appease you, so button your lip and let's get ready to ride. I want to reach that campfire I saw by late this evening."

Molly didn't say another word but marched over to saddle and bridle her horse, leaving Longarm to break camp, empty the coffee pot and pack up their bedrolls. She finished saddling and was ready to ride ten minutes before he was. They were both angry as they took to the trail. It was, Longarm thought, a bad beginning to what could be a long and difficult day.

"What do you think?" she asked him as they dismounted and led their horses into a small box canyon. "Are we close to their camp?"

"No more than a mile. Are you up to a moonlight hike?"

"I sure am. If it's them, are you really going to give them a chance to surrender?"

"That's the general idea."

"Custis, if we do that they will scatter and surround us in the dark. We won't last until midnight."

Longarm shook his head. "Are you always this way, or are you just trying to make things seem as bad as possible?"

"I . . . look, I'm sorry. And I will follow your orders."

"Promise?"

"Yes. I gave you my word, didn't I?"

"That's right," he said, "I just wanted to make sure that you remembered."

"Well, I do, so let's stop jawing and start walking."

Longarm set off with his rifle in hand while Molly carried her shotgun. They had both seen the campfire light only a short time ago, so he knew that whoever he'd seen last evening hadn't moved. Now it was simply a matter of finding out what they were up against and then making correct decisions.

They followed an arroyo the last quarter of a mile, and Longarm was careful to approach the camp from downwind, just in case there were dog. When they drew nearer, he eased up from the arroyo and surveyed the camp from close range.

"Indians," he said. "I count six."

"And whites. Look! There's four of them off by themselves."

"You're right," Longarm replied. "Do you think these are Navajo or Hopi?"

"Definitely Navajo. We're in trouble, Custis. They say Indians can see in the dark."

"That's not true. At least, not in my experience."

"What are we going to do?"

"I don't know yet."

"They've got cattle and quite a few horses. And look! That's a woman tending the fire!"

"I wonder if she's there of her own free will or not?"

"I'll bet she's a captive!"

Molly's voice caused Longarm to turn away from the campfire, and he leaned close to Molly, whispering, "Just control yourself. These could be law-abiding men."

"Way out here in Indian country?"

"Shhh! Not so loud." Longarm sank back out of sight and considered his next move. He could feel Molly's eyes boring into him, and she fidgeted with impatience.

"Okay," he said, "we'll wait until they go to sleep. It might be well after midnight, but we'll be patient. Then, when they are all asleep, we'll sneak in from opposite sides of their camp and disarm them."

"What if they post a sentry?"

"Because this country is so empty, I don't expect that."

"But what if they do?"

"Then I'll sneak down and try to get the drop on him. If this is part of the Four Corners Gang and the sentry goes for his gun, I'll kill him."

"That's the *best* idea you can come up with?"

"You got a better one?"

"Sure, why don't we just stand up with our guns in our hands and order them to freeze?"

"Because, if they're outlaws, they wouldn't, and then we'd be facing too many guns," Longarm reasoned. "So let's do this my way and maybe no one will be killed. I'm not going to take the chance of opening fire on innocent men."

"I'll bet anything that they're not innocent," Molly warned. "And that they'll put up a fight."

"If they do, shoot to kill."

"All right."

Longarm gave her arm a squeeze and then said, "I'm going to circle their camp and come in from the other side."

"How will I know—"

"You'll see my silhouette when I stand up, and then we'll both advance at the same time. But Molly, don't make a move until you see me, no matter how much time passes. I'm not coming in on them until I'm sure that they're asleep."

"I understand. Good luck, Custis."

"The same to you."

It took Longarm nearly an hour to circle the camp and find a good vantage point. He hunkered down to wait and wonder what would happen next.

59

The moon highlighted the distant Hopi mesas, which reminded Longarm of three huge ships emerging from behind an ocean fog. After a while the moon ducked behind clouds, and then Longarm could see almost nothing except the campfire. When the moon finally did reappear, he noted that everyone had retired to their bedroll except the woman, who sat wrapped in a blanket staring at the fire. He gave her another two whole hours, but she was still awake and even occasionally fed the fire to keep it alive.

Longarm yawned and he stared at the Hopi mesas, then over to where he knew Molly was hiding. He feared she would grow impatient and act on her own if the woman below did not finally go to sleep.

If she is a captive, she probably has been worked into exhaustion and won't be aware of my approach. With luck, I can silence her until she understands that we mean to rescue her from these men. But what if she is not a captive?

As the long night began to ebb, Longarm knew that he had to act without further delay. He started quietly forward toward the woman who was, fortunately, facing away from him and seemed mesmerized by the flames. Longarm advanced until he was among the sleeping men, and then he saw Molly coming forward with her shotgun.

The woman saw Molly first and started to jump to her feet. Longarm took three quick strides and clamped his left hand over her mouth and then whispered, ''We're friends. Don't scream. We have come to help.''

The woman froze and Longarm added, ''Are these men outlaws?''

''Yes,'' she breathed when he loosened his grip. ''The white men are killers.''

''And the Indians?''

''They bring horses, food and water in exchange for money, weapons and whiskey.''

Longarm threw up his left hand and hoped that Molly could see that he wanted her to stop. She understood and rooted herself not twenty feet away, so Longarm whispered,

"Go to my friend and tell her to take you to safety! Hurry!"

The poor young woman was alert enough not to awaken any of the sleeping men as she crossed the camp and joined Molly. Longarm saw their heads lean close, and then the pair of women turned and started to hurry away. Everything was going just fine until one of the outlaws got up and staggered toward a water barrel.

"Hey," he muttered, still half asleep as he finally noticed Longarm standing with a rifle in his fists, "who are you?"

"A friend in need," Longarm said, striding forward toward the man and hoping he would not awaken sufficiently to sound the alarm.

But Longarm's hopes were in vain. The outlaw muttered something and slapped his side as if to reach for his gun. Only he'd left it by his bedroll. Confused but waking up fast, he lunged for his six-gun with an oath on his lips.

Longarm didn't actually see the shocked outlaw cock and lift his six-gun, but this was no time for taking chances, so he slashed downward with his rifle barrel. The outlaw's pistol fired harmlessly into the dirt as his skull cracked like an eggshell, killing him instantly. The other outlaws sat up fast, reaching for their guns. Feeling more comfortable at close range with a pistol, Longarm dropped the rifle and made his cross draw. Six-gun in hand, he concentrated on making every shot count. A bullet grazed his temple and sent his hat flying. Longarm staggered and shot the last outlaw twice, knocking him over backwards.

"Custis!"

"The Navajos!" he shouted. "Molly, watch out for them!"

But the Indians were far more interested in making tracks than corpses. Longarm saw their fleeting shadows vanish into the brush as they fled for their lives.

"Custis!"

"I'm all right," he answered, reloading in a crouched

position so that he was not an easy target if one of the outlaws was still alive. "Stay back!"

But Molly rushed across the camp and threw herself at Longarm, causing them both to collapse in the dirt.

"Molly, get off me until we know for sure it's safe!"

Breaking loose from her grip, he heard a moaning sound and crabbed over to an outlaw and made sure he wasn't holding a weapon.

"I'm dyin'!"

"Where are you hit?"

"In the guts."

Longarm brushed his fingers across the man's shirt and felt warm, welling blood.

"I'll get you over to the fire; maybe you aren't hit as bad as you think. Hold on."

Longarm half-dragged, half-carried the outlaw to the campfire shouting, "Molly, get some more wood on this fire!"

There was a pile of wood close at hand, and the captive woman helped Molly feed the low flames until Longarm had a clear vision of the wounded outlaw. The man appeared to be in his thirties but might have been a lot younger. Riding the outlaw trail and always being on the run prematurely aged men. He was tall and thin with a black beard and mustache. If his face hadn't been twisted with pain, he probably would have been considered handsome.

"Who . . . who are you!" he managed to gasp.

"Deputy Marshal Custis Long. Who are you?"

"I'm dead!" the man wailed. "And so will you be when my brothers find out you kilt me!"

"Are you one of the Hooker brothers?"

The dying man's reply was a strangled curse.

"Where are the others in your gang?"

The outlaw struggled to spit in Longarm's face, but just expelled his dying breath. His fingers lifted toward Longarm's throat, but strength failed him, and he died with a long rattling sound.

Longarm went to check on the other three outlaws who were all dead.

"You killed them *all*," Molly whispered with amazement. "Four men and you killed every last one."

"I had a big advantage over the first three," Longarm informed her. "None of them was fully awake. But the last man was very good."

"You've been hit," the captive woman said, touching the side of his head.

"It's nothing," Longarm replied, suddenly feeling woozy. "See if you can find whiskey and bandaging."

"I'll find both," the woman promised, hurrying over to a pile of supplies and quickly rummaging up a bottle and a clean shirt, which she tore into strips.

"It's just a crease," she told him. "You aren't going to bleed to death or anything, so don't get upset."

"I won't."

Longarm slumped beside the campfire and helped himself to a pull on the whiskey. It was better than he'd expected, so he helped himself to another generous swallow while the woman doused her bandaging and then wrapped the whiskey-soaked strips around his head like a turban.

"Ouch! That really stings."

"I'm sorry. I heard you tell Race before he died that you were a federal marshal. Did you come all the way out here to save me?"

"No, but I'm glad we could help. Who are you?"

"My name is Lucy Taylor. I was taken by force from a train about a month ago."

"I read about you in Flagstaff," he said. "I'm surprised you are still alive."

"There were times that I wished I was . . . dead!" Lucy's shoulders began to shake and she struggled not to break down in tears.

"Lucy, I know it's hard," Longarm said, "but I have to

63

ask you one more question. Will those Indians return with others to kill us?''

"Maybe not."

"But maybe so?"

"I . . . I can't say. They didn't talk in English, and I have no idea where they came from or where they've gone."

"Were they Navajo?"

"Yes."

"Molly, I don't feel much like moving, but I think we're going to have to right away. We can't take the chance that those Navajo will return with a bunch of friends and seek revenge."

"But where can we hide?"

Longarm raised the whiskey bottle and pointed northward. "I think we had better acquaint ourselves with this country's only peaceable people."

"The Hopi?"

"That's right. The farmers who live on the three high mesas."

Molly nodded in solemn agreement. "We don't have much choice, do we?"

"Not if we want to see another sundown."

"I'll go back and get our horses."

Longarm took another drink, but then he corked the bottle and said, "Lucy, are you strong enough to help us gather up everything here and get packed and ready?"

"Yes."

"Good. Everything is going to be all right. I promise we'll get you out of this country alive."

Lucy choked back her tears, hugged Longarm's neck and then scurried off to make preparations.

"I feel so sorry for her," Molly said. "Because we've both suffered at the hands of this gang."

"Lean on each other and grow strong."

"What about the bodies of those four outlaws?"

"Are you asking me if I want to bury them?"

"I guess that is exactly what I'm asking."

"I never bury vermin."

Molly nodded with understanding. "I'll get our horses. We can leave within the hour."

"I'm going to need to close my eyes and sleep for a few minutes. I feel a little . . . unsteady." Longarm stretched out beside the fire, and, before he fell asleep, Lucy covered him with a blanket.

"You were amazing," she whispered. "And I will never, *ever* forget this night if I live to be eighty. You're my hero."

"Don't get too carried away," he warned with a yawn. "We're not out of the woods yet."

"What woods?"

It was a joke, but neither of them laughed as Longarm closed his gritty eyes and fell asleep.

Chapter 7

Longarm didn't know much about Hopi Indians except that they were said to be farmers rather than hunters and were surrounded by their traditional enemies, the far more numerous Navajo. He also knew that they lived atop three high mesas that jutted out over this lower high desert country at an altitude of over five thousand feet. Neither Lucy nor Molly had ever been on the Hopi mesas, but this morning Longarm could see the silhouette of one of their mesatop villages.

"I expect I had better ride up toward that mesa alone and wait for them to come down and talk," he mused aloud.

"Maybe that won't be necessary," Molly replied.

"Why not?"

"Because I think I see Hopi farmers in their corn fields about a mile to the east."

Longarm reined his horse in their direction, wondering if the Hopi would be alarmed by their approach. When they were within a mile of the Indians, he reined up and said, "You ladies wait here with the horses and the gear while I speak to these people."

"I ought to come along with you," Lucy argued. "The Hopi have seen me already, and that could ease things."

"Okay then," Longarm agreed. "Will they speak English?"

Lucy nodded. "There have been missionaries for the last few centuries, and now I'm sure they have been assigned Indian agents. At the very least, some of the leaders will speak English."

"Good."

"Now wait just a minute here," Molly protested, "I don't much appreciate being left behind."

"It won't be for long," Custis promised as he pushed his horse into an easy lope toward the cornfields.

The Hopi saw him and collected at the border of their fields. They were short, stocky men with straight black hair falling down to their shoulders. With few exceptions, they wore cotton trousers and shirts, although some were bare chested. He noted that all of these people were barefooted.

"I sure hope this goes well," Longarm said as he slowed his horse to a walk and raised his left hand in the traditional sign of greeting.

"Smile," Lucy urged.

Longarm smiled, and the half dozen Hopi smiled back.

"Friend!" Longarm declared loudly. "I am a United States Marshal."

When this elicited no response, Longarm fumbled for his badge and then held it up for them to see. "Marshal. I come in peace."

"Who is your friend?" one of the older men who wore a calico shirt and cloth headband asked in slow but flawless English.

"Her name is Lucy."

"I know this woman. She was with the bad men."

"They are dead," Longarm announced. "I have their horses, guns and supplies. We need help before other bad men come to avenge the ones I killed."

The leader turned to his companions and translated this information. There was a brief discussion, and then the leader turned to Longarm. "We do not want more trouble with the Navajo or Hooker men."

"I did not kill or harm any Navajo," Longarm explained. "I took this woman, who was a slave. She needs your help, just as I do."

"And what about the horses?" a second man asked, pointing back to Molly and the outlaws' saddled horses.

"They belonged to Hooker men, but you can have them if you help us."

"How come you ride with only women?"

"Long story," Custis replied. "But I ask only that you give us shelter for a few days in exchange for those Hooker horses, saddles and guns."

"How many horses and saddles?"

"Seven good horses," Lucy answered, "five saddles."

"United States Marshal go back to horses and we will talk," the one with the headband decided aloud.

Longarm nodded with agreement. "We need help and are willing to pay."

"Marshal go after Hooker gang?"

"Yes."

"With two women?" the Hopi asked, not bothering to mask his skepticism.

"No," Longarm corrected. "This woman would stay here with you until I return. Other woman come with me to fight Hooker men."

The Hopi shook his head. "One marshal. One woman against Hooker men? You no come back ever."

"If I don't come back," Longarm said, "you can keep this woman as your wife."

"What!" Lucy screeched. "Are you crazy!"

"Shhh," Longarm hissed. "Lucy, I'm trying real hard to work a deal here that will help you."

"Help me!" Lucy shouted. "I'm never going to be anyone's slave or captive again! I won't."

"Marshal, you take this noisy white woman with you," the Hopi leader decided. "We no want."

"But . . ."

"Leave Hooker horses, guns. Nothing else."

"In return for what?" Longarm demanded. "Chief, I—"

"Name is Chief Tevesaya," the Hopi corrected. "You not happy with my words, then go away now. Hopi no need white man's trouble. Hopi need only rain for corn."

Longarm stared into the square, determined face of the leader and knew that there would be no bartering. "All right," he sighed. "I'll take both women, but I want a guide to lead us to the Hooker gang."

"Big ranch," the Hopi said, turning to point northeast. "Not possible to miss even for white man who only rides with women."

Longarm ignored the thinly veiled insult. "Chief Tevesaya, this is a dry and hard country."

"Hopi land is *good* land!"

"Sure, but it is pretty dry and with all these canyons, buttes and mountains, it is hard to travel and easy for the enemy to set an ambush. Chief Tevesaya, we really need a guide to lead us."

"Navajo catch and kill Hopi guide. Maybe also kill you and take woman, horses, guns!"

"I realize the danger, but there is no choice. The Four Corners Gang, led by the Hookers, have killed and hurt too many people and must be stopped. Brought to a white man's judge if possible but, if not, shot to death so that they can raid no more. Wouldn't you like to be rid of them, too?"

"Hooker gang bad, bad men. They come and take Hopi corn sometimes. Take Hopi women, too! Kill Hopi if we fight."

"Then you ought to try to help me rid this country of them. All I ask is for one guide, and we will give him a good horse so that, if there is bad trouble, he can return to your people. Other than that, I want nothing but a night of rest and some water to fill our keg and canteens so that we and our horses suffer no more. This is fair, and I will ask no more of the Hopi.''

"You take *both* women."

"Now wait a minute," Longarm protested.

But Chief Tevesaya was firm. "Indian agent not like them to stay with Hopi. Besides, they no good at grinding corn."

"You got *that* right," Lucy crowed.

"Chief—"

"No, take woman!"

"Okay, dammit," Longarm snapped, not daring any more argument. "I'll take both women."

"Marshal go away now while Hopi talk."

Longarm and Lucy rode back to join Molly. Lucy was furious and said, "Do you know what this . . . this man said to the Hopi?"

"No," Molly said, "but I expect you'll tell me."

"He was willing to give me to them as a slave wife if you didn't return! And that old chief would probably have taken me if I knew how to grind corn!"

Molly shot Longarm a withering glance. "Lucy, it only proves we have to stick together, or Custis will sell us down the river."

Longarm groaned, then dismounted and sought out the shade of a pinion pine. Untying a bedroll from the back of his saddle, he spread it out on the ground, using every inch of shade that could be found and stretched out to take a nap.

"You're going to sleep *again*?" Molly asked.

"Yep."

"What's the matter with you, Custis? You got the sleeping sickness or something?"

"Nope. I just know a thing or two about Indians."

"Such as?"

"They don't come to decisions quickly or easily. It will probably be hours before they agree on how to handle my proposition. We might as well enjoy a nap."

Longarm yawned, pulled his hat over his eyes and fell asleep almost instantly.

"Wake up," Molly said, gently nudging Longarm with the toe of her boot. "We've got visitors."

Longarm sat up, realizing that the sun was low on the western horizon. He yawned and turned around to see all six of the Hopi farmers watching him with amusement.

"Marshal sleep in daytime too?" Chief Tevesaya asked.

"Only when I'm tired."

"We will help you," the chief announced. "Come to village but keep women quiet and no fighting."

"That's fair enough. What about a guide?"

"He come soon."

"Can he shoot straight?" Molly asked.

The chief cast her a withering glance. "Shoot good. Not like woman."

Molly's cheeks turned red with anger. "Watch this, Chief!"

"No!" Longarm shouted.

But Molly drew her six-gun and fired three times, exploding small cones off a pinion pine.

"Holy cow!" Lucy whispered.

"You said it," Chief Tevesaya solemnly added. "You sure you woman?"

"We'd better get moving," Longarm said, taking Molly's arm before she exploded in anger. "It appears that we have a pretty good climb up to those mesa-top pueblos."

It was a long and difficult climb up a winding path to the Hopi mesa. Because of the altitude, their horses were really puffing by the time they arrived at an ancient village perched on a narrow finger of rock hundreds of feet over the mesa below.

"Good heavens!" Molly exclaimed as they crested the mesa top and stared at the three- and four-story high col-

71

lection of crumbling pueblos, many of them hanging right on the very edge of the mesa itself, looking as if they were ready to tumble off the cliffs and go crashing to the desert floor far below. "I would never have believed that such places as this still exist. Custis, have you ever—"

"No," he said, awed by the sight of the towering pueblos and the curious villagers who now began to appear. "This is like stepping back a thousand years. I've seen cliff dwellings before, but they were always long abandoned. These people must be their modern descendants."

A naked boy of about five smiled at them, and his puppy, a spotted mongrel with one ear up and the other dropping, wagged its tail. A very, very old man with a carved walking stick emerged from a dim underground dwelling and stared at Longarm for several moments before he lost interest and went to inspect their horses. Other Hopi slowly appeared, and soon the small plaza on the edge of the soaring mesa was filled.

"Custis, what happens now?" Molly asked.

"I guess we just stand here until they tire of us and then we find a place to sleep and eat."

"Look at that pretty girl," Lucy said, pointing.

"She's cute all right," Longarm agreed, noting a child of about twelve with luminous black eyes. She wore a silver necklace and white cotton dress adorned with colorful kernels of corn sewn into the fabric.

Chief Tevesaya reappeared with a silver-haired man of great dignity, who was introduced as Nahota. Longarm did not even attempt to judge the man's age. He was about five-foot-eight and had a deeply lined face.

"Chief Nahota was the one who agreed that you and the women could stay here with us," Tevesaya explained.

"You mean that someone from the fields ran all the way up here to ask if he would do this?"

"After we decide in the fields, then we ask Nahota."

Longarm removed his hat in a sign of respect. "Chief

72

Nahota, I am grateful to you for letting us enter your village. We will leave tomorrow."

"You stay two days."

Longarm didn't even consider arguing. All the other Hopi men, women and children had fallen silent, and someone in the background was translating the conversation for them in Hopi.

"What about our guide?"

"He will come soon."

"Good," Longarm replied, wondering if their guide was saying prayers in anticipation of dying. "I promise no harm will come to him."

"He is not afraid of death. Are you?"

Longarm hedged by answering, "I'd prefer not to get killed."

"And your women?"

"We feel the same," Lucy said, looking to Molly, who nodded vigorously.

"Are you the woman who shoots like a man?" Nahota asked, eyes boring into Molly.

"Yes, but—"

"Wrong for woman to shoot like man. Can you grind corn?"

"No."

"Not worth much then to Hopi man."

To her credit, Molly didn't argue with the old chief but instead clenched her jaw in angry silence.

"We feed and water horses now," Tevesaya announced. "Then we eat."

"Good," Longarm replied, "because I am mighty hungry."

An hour passed, and the Hopi villagers lost interest in their visitors, so Longarm and his female companions unsaddled and spread out their bedrolls in the little plaza. They could hear the steady grinding of Hopi women at work on their metates, and when the shadows grew long, they mixed the corn meal with water to create a thin bluish

73

colored dough which they spread out on flat baking rocks. This resulted in delicious tortillas called piki, which Longarm consumed in great quantities. Molly and Lucy also seemed to enjoy the Hopi staple, and it was dark when they were finished eating. They watched as the old men and younger boys retired to a circular underground room by way of a ladder thrust through the roof.

"I wonder what they do down there?" Molly asked.

"They live, sleep and hold ceremonies," Lucy informed them. "Those places are called 'kivas'."

Longarm was surprised at her knowledge. "How do you know that?"

"Because the Hooker men were talking about the Hopi. They said that these people are very religious."

"Why do you think we have to stay two days?" Molly asked just as Longarm was about to fall asleep.

"I have no idea. Maybe our guide needs a little time to prepare himself for the journey."

"Maybe we don't even need a guide," Lucy said. "I'll bet we could locate the Four Corners Gang without help."

"I'm sure we could, but would someone find us first?"

"Are you talking about the Hookers?"

"Or Navajo intent on stealing our horses," Longarm told her. "Now why don't we quit talking and just go to sleep."

They slept well that night and awoke to the sound of prayers being sung by a Hopi crier who then tossed corn meal to the four winds. The village came awake with the rising of the sun, and nothing much happened that day. Longarm, Molly and Lucy wandered around, and the people seemed friendly, but shy and aloof. They were treated with respect but did not see either their guide or the two elder chiefs.

"I wonder where they went," Longarm asked the second evening as they again feasted on piki and readied themselves for sleep.

"Maybe they are involved in some kind of religious ceremony," Lucy offered.

Molly nodded. "I'll bet you're right. They're probably praying that our guide returns safely. I'm anxious to meet him."

"I expect we will, first thing tomorrow morning," Longarm told them as he lit a cigar and stretched out on his bedroll to gaze up at the starry sky.

The next morning they were awakened as usual by the crier offering to the rising sun. But now drums beat and soon a procession of old men emerged from the depths of a large, circular kiva.

"Here we go," Longarm whispered, seeing Chief Nahota in the lead followed by Tevesaya and several other Hopi elders.

The procession encircled them, and the drum beat and chanting began as Nahota looked deeply into Longarm's eyes as if he could see into his soul. "We have offered many prayers for you."

"I appreciate that, Chief Nahota."

"May you fight well and greet death with honor."

"I sure don't—"

"Redbow," the chief called, turning to the kiva.

Everyone looked that way, and slowly a tall young man emerged from the ceremonial chamber. Longarm blinked with surprise because Redbow was a remarkable physical specimen of manhood. He was as tall as Longarm, although not quite as muscular. He moved like a cat, and his black hair bore a reddish cast, while his nose was hooked like the beak of a hawk.

"I never saw a Hopi that looked like *him*," Lucy whispered.

"He's a half-breed." Longarm told her.

Their guide wore a thick buckskin hunting jacket decorated with red beads. Redbow was armed with two pistols, a Bowie knife and a hunting bow that must have been six feet long.

75

"Isn't he handsome?" Molly said under her breath. "I've never seen anyone like him before."

"He sure is," Lucy agreed.

Redbow didn't seem to notice the two admiring women as he came to stand before Longarm. "You are a marshal?"

"I am. Who are you?"

"Redbow."

"I know your name," Longarm said, peering into eyes that showed no emotion whatsoever. "What I want to know is who you are, and why were you chosen."

"I have a destiny," Redbow told him. "And it is to help you kill the men you seek."

Longarm turned on his heel to Nahota. "I wanted a guide, not an assassin."

"Redbow will do as you say."

"Is that right?" Longarm turned back to the half-breed. "What did the men I seek do to you?"

"It does not matter to you."

"No, I suppose it doesn't," Longarm replied. "But whatever it was, you want to even the score."

"Without me, you and the women will die."

Longarm took a deep breath. "I don't think so. Chief Nahota?"

The chief stepped between them, and Longarm said, "I asked for a Hopi guide. I do not want this man."

"Redbow will protect you."

"I can protect myself."

"Can you protect these woman as well?" the chief asked.

"Custis," Molly pleaded, "we need all the help we can get!"

"She's right," Lucy agreed. "We can come to an understanding later. This is no time to be proud."

If he had been alone, Longarm would have left this village. But he was not alone, and they did need all the help they could get, so he reluctantly nodded his head in agreement and snapped, "All right then, let's go."

In reply, Chief Nahota placed one hand on Longarm's shoulder and the other on that of Redbow. "You must never fight."

Longarm followed the chief's reasoning because he had a feeling that Redbow would be a terrible opponent if they ever crossed each other. He had fought some hard men in his time and bore the scars to prove it, but he'd never looked into such a deadly pair of eyes.

"Too much time has passed and too many words have been spoken," Redbow said to Longarm.

"I agree."

So they gathered their horses, and the Hopi people gave them food and prayers. Down off the mesa they came and then, without a word, Redbow began to run.

"Doesn't he even want a horse?" Lucy asked, looking bewildered.

"It sure doesn't look like it," Longarm said as their tall, lithe guide set a hard pace through the brush, never once glancing back to see if he was being followed.

"We'd better get moving," Molly warned, "or he'll lose us."

Longarm twisted around in the saddle and gazed up at the Hopi mesa. He could see people lined up along the cliff, watching. Shaking his head, he growled, "This is the damnedest deal I ever saw, but I guess we had better play the hand they've dealt us and follow Redbow."

So they whipped their mounts into a gallop and rode hard after their new guide, all three wondering what on earth was going to happen next.

Chapter 8

As they rode north following the tireless half-breed, a host of new questions formed in Longarm's mind. Not only did he now wonder how many of the Four Corners Gang he would have to face, but also what kind of a man they were following. He had heard of long-distance Indian runners and knew that the Apache were especially noted for this remarkable ability. In the arid Southwest where both grass and water was at a premium, the Apache, Pima and apparently the Hopi as well had learned that livestock were often a burden. And so, these peoples preferred to *eat* horses, burros and mules rather than to constantly struggle with attempting to find them food and water. Longarm had heard stories of how the Apache in particular could travel on foot all day and night, covering up to sixty or seventy miles in a single epic marathon. It was this ability that had made the Apache so difficult to subdue by the United States Army.

This, however, was the first time that Longarm had actually witnessed such a feat of running, and as the long day of mostly uphill climbing grew to an end, he was amazed by Redbow's incredible endurance. Their horses were fit, but no match for the half-breed who was sometimes forced to stop and wait for them to catch up. The man wore thick woven sandals and covered the ground with phenomenal strides that did not vary even on the uphill or through heavy brush and rocks.

All morning they seemed to flank the Hopi mesas until they were to the west and the south, barely visible in the clear, high, desert air. In the afternoon they traversed a long, dry valley for at least twenty miles before the sun slipped into the western horizon. Even then Redbow might have continued into the darkness, except that Lucy and Molly refused to go any farther.

"Enough," Lucy pleaded. "We don't have to reach Four Corners in one day!"

Longarm had to spur his flagging mount hard to overtake Redbow and explain that it was time to stop and rest.

"There is a spring up ahead," the tall man said, barely breathing hard. "We stop there for the night."

"Fine," Longarm agreed. "We'll catch up."

Redbow started to say something more, but then changed his mind and began running again. He concentrated on his breathing as well as the smoothness of his stride and took pleasure in knowing that his footsteps were soft and sure. The sky was brilliant with sunset when he neared the spring and smelled a campfire. The half-breed swung up a deep arroyo and finally slowed to a walk, drawing an arrow from his quiver and fitting it to the gut string of his long bow. Moving forward as silently as a ghost, he scaled the arroyo and slipped into a stand of pines and gazed down at the three men camped below.

Were they outlaws who rode for his enemies, the Hookers? Men who preyed upon the weak and defenseless and would cut a man's throat for a swallow of whiskey?

Redbow knew that he did not have much time to find out before the marshal and his women barged into view. At best, he had ten minutes to decide if these were friends or enemies, but not a second longer. If these men were killers, they would reach for their rifles and probably ambush the marshal and the two white women who foolishly dared to enter this country without knowing of its deadly secrets.

Redbow checked his pistols and Bowie knife to make sure that they were properly placed and in easy reach. His black eyes narrowed, and he studied each face until his broad shoulders sagged with disappointment. The old one that he had vowed to kill slowly was not among these three. No matter, these men probably worked for him, so killing them would be almost as satisfying. He raised his bow and began to draw back the long, iron-tipped arrow, remembering . . .

"If we could sneak up on 'em and open fire with our rifles," one of the men said, "we could kill three of the gang right now. And then, when the others came rushing out to see what was going on, we could kill another three or four. That ought to get us that big reward."

"Sure," another argued, "but what if there are twenty or thirty? We can't kill that many before they kill us! And you know that old Yancy Hooker isn't going to rest until he peels our hides like the skin off an apple."

"I don't know," the third one said, shaking his head. "My feeling is that, if we sneak up and find out there's just too damn many to kill in one volley, then we just ought to clear out of this country and forget the whole deal."

"I ain't come this far to ride out of this country with nothing to show for it."

"You think I want to quit!"

"That's how it sounds."

"Well, Bert, I don't! But none of us wants to die, either! That was the agreement, remember? If there's too many, then we ride away quiet so they never knew we came."

Redbow eased up the pressure on his bow and retreated back into the gathering darkness. He removed his arrow from its bowstring and replaced it in his quiver. These were simply more fools after the reward and were, therefore, probably destined to find death by their own hands. Redbow slipped back into the arroyo and ran quietly until he met the marshal and the women.

"There are white men up at the spring," he announced.

"Outlaws?" Longarm asked.

"No, fools after the reward."

"How many?"

"Three."

Longarm dismounted and handed his reins to Molly, saying, "Redbow and I will go to meet them on foot. We'll call when it's safe to ride in."

"All right," Molly agreed.

It felt good to get out of the saddle and walk a bit, but Longarm knew that there was a danger in this encounter. A lot of bounty hunters were nothing but trigger-happy fools who shot first and asked questions later. "Redbow?"

"Yes?"

"We need to be careful how we approach them, or we could find ourselves dodging bullets. So let's just sneak in, and when we are close, I'll stand up suddenly and announce than I'm a United States Marshal. Can you use those pistols you wear?"

"I can."

"Well, I hope you won't have to, but these boys are bound to be pretty spooked out here in this wild country, so let's just step easy and try not to surprise them too bad."

Longarm took Redbow's silence as agreement and added, "You know the layout of their camp, so you lead and I'll follow."

The half-breed whirled around and took off at a run, leaving Longarm no choice but to do the same. He sure hoped that the men were camped nearby, or Redbow was going to make him look bad. As a youngster, Longarm had been the fastest kid in his county and had never been bested in a foot race, but he wasn't young anymore and even then he'd considered himself a sprinter.

They ran up a shadowy arroyo for nearly half a mile, and Longarm's breath started coming in bursts. If silence hadn't been required, he'd have shouted at the half-breed to slow the hell down, but that wasn't an option now, so he tried to keep from sounding like a wind-broken horse. Thankfully, Redbow came to a halt and then motioned to indicate they were supposed to climb the bank of the arroyo.

"Okay," Longarm panted, "just give me a moment to catch my breath."

"Marshal soft," Redbow grunted.

"Maybe I am, but I got enough in me to handle you," Longarm warned. "So don't get any ideas about who is in charge."

In reply, Redbow fitted his bowstring and glared at Longarm.

"Listen," Longarm said, trying hard to avoid a confrontation, "if these three fellas are worth a damn, maybe we can use their help."

"No good."

"Let me be the judge of that, okay?" Longarm was fast running out of patience, and he attacked the side of the arroyo. Unfortunately, a large rock turned under his foot and bounced noisily until it came to rest at the bottom.

"Dammit!" Longarm hissed, struggling up to the top and peering down at an abandoned campfire. "Dammit, they heard me and took cover."

He clenched his fist in self-disgust, took a deep breath and shouted, "My name is Custis Long and I'm a—"

Longarm never got to finish his introduction because the bounty hunters opened up with their rifles. Longarm threw himself to one side, but not before a slug kicked dirt and rock shards into his face. Momentarily blinded, he rolled twice, one hand going to cover his eye and the other dragging out his six-gun.

"Redbow, are you all right?" he asked.

There was no answer. The half-breed was gone.

"Hold your fire!" Longarm shouted, even as he heard the whirring sound of an arrow cutting through the air.

A man screamed in a way that Longarm had learned meant death.

"Redbow!"

Longarm heard more rifle fire and then he heard curses, the sound of flesh striking flesh followed by another dying scream. Seconds later, a grunt and then what sounded like a wounded animal thrashing in the forest.

"Redbow, gawdamnit! Where are you?"

"I am here to see if you look."

Longarm crabbed forward until he had a clear view of the campfire. He saw Redbow with the Bowie knife clenched in one fist and a pistol in the other. Two men lay twisted at his feet, unmoving.

Longarm removed his hand from his eye, but his vision was blurred. He hoped that he'd not suffered a permanent eye injury because, given the circumstances, that could prove to be as fatal to him as Redbow had been to the motionless pair at his feet.

"What happened?" he asked, stumbling down to the campfire.

"They chose to fight instead of listen."

An angry response formed in Longarm's mouth, but he choked it off and instead asked, "You said that there were three. Where is the last man?"

"He ran for his life like a coward. We do not need him."

"Is he wounded?"

"Yes."

"But still alive?"

"I don't know."

"Well find out and . . . Redbow, can I trust you not to finish him off?"

The half-breed struggled with his emotions and only then did Longarm notice a stream of blood welling from a bullet hole in his right leg spaced about halfway between the hip and the knee.

"Sit down," Longarm ordered, "while I take a look at that gunshot."

"No."

"Dammit, if the bullet is still in your leg, it has to come out!"

Redbow's response was to pivot around so that Longarm saw the bullet's exit hole where his flesh was torn outward.

"Molly! Lucy! Come quick!" he shouted. Then, turning to their guide, Longarm took off his bandanna and tied it firmly around the wound, saying, "Redbow, I'm ordering you to sit here and not move! The last thing you need is to lose so much blood that we have to throw you across the back of a horse and try to get you to your Hopi people."

"They are not my people. They are my friends."

"Let's not split hairs, okay? Just relax. You've killed two men who ought to be alive and able to help us when we come up against the Hooker bunch. And, unless I miss my guess, you've probably killed the third one as well."

Redbow's silence did nothing to change that opinion. Longarm blinked hard, willing his eye to return to normal. When it didn't, he spied a canteen, uncorked it and drenched the eye to return to normal. After a few moments, he was greatly relieved when his full vision returned.

"Which way did the wounded one run?"

Redbow pointed to the east, and Longarm scowled with displeasure. "If you hadn't gotten yourself plugged, I'd send you out into the dark after him."

Longarm did not receive an answer, so he headed out in pursuit of a man he figured was either mortally wounded or already dead.

Chapter 9

Longarm wasn't a bit pleased about having to go off in the dark searching for a wounded bounty hunter. If the man was still alive, he'd be in a mood to fight, not talk. But Longarm couldn't, in good conscience, allow a wounded man to suffer and die if his life could be saved, so there really was no choice.

The moon was a bright wedge in the sky, and the stars were brilliant, so he had some light to see by as he stalked through the brush and the rocks with a gun held tight in his fist.

"Hello up there!" he called again and again. "I'm a United States Marshal. If you're wounded, I can help!"

Finally, he heard a low moan and called, "Mister, do you need help?"

"I got an arrow in my back!"

"I'm coming, but don't shoot! Do you hear me?"

"Yeah." The wounded bounty hunter sobbed. "Hurry up, Marshal! I'm bleeding to death!"

Longarm moved quickly, but he had learned the hard way not to trust anyone, so he kept his gun ready. When he saw the man sprawled face down in a dry wash, he hesitated a moment and then ordered, "Push your hands out from your sides!"

"Huh?" he asked weakly.

"You heard me! Hands out so I know you're unarmed!"

The man complied, so Longarm hurried to his aid. The very first thing he saw was the shaft of Redbow's arrow protruding from his back, just below the shoulder blade.

"Hold real still," Longarm ordered an instant before he snapped off the shaft and threw it away.

"Oww! Am I dyin'?"

"I don't know," Longarm said honestly. "Why the hell did you and your friends open fire?"

"We thought you were the Four Corners Gang!"

"Fatal mistake. Are you hit anywhere else?"

"No. But gawd it hurts!"

"I need to get you back to the campfire and see if we can remove the arrow. It won't be easy, but you'll bleed to death if we don't try."

"All right." The man expelled a ragged breath. "But Marshal, if I don't make it, my name is Andy Drew, and I'm from Tucson. Got that?"

"Yeah."

"I got both folks livin' down in Tucson. You let 'em know I got killed by an Indian. Okay?"

"Stop talking about dying and try to help me save your life."

"Okay, but you wouldn't leave my body out here for the vultures and coyotes to eat, would you?"

"No."

"Sir, if I die, bury me deep, and tell my folks their Andy boy died trying to earn that bounty money to help 'em out in their old age."

"Save your breath, Andy. You might just need it."

"Yes sir. I think I'm a goner."

Longarm helped the man to his feet. The bounty hunter moaned and momentarily lost consciousness, so Longarm had no choice but to hoist him up and carry him back to the campfire.

Molly was attending to Redbow's wound, so Lucy came

86

over to help Longarm. "Custis, is he already dead?"

"Just passed out. We've got to remove the arrowhead and see if we can stop the bleeding."

Molly shot an accusing glance at Redbow. "You put an arrow in his *back*?"

"It happened fast," the half-breed replied.

"There's no time for talk," Longarm said tersely. "Let's try to get the arrow out before Andy awakens."

Longarm grabbed the stubby shaft and gently pulled, but the arrowhead refused to budge. "Molly, I'm going to have to cut it out. Lucy, it would help if you threw some more wood on the fire. I'll need all the light I can get."

"Can't you just leave it until morning?" Molly asked.

"He'd be dead by then. Pin his arms in case he comes awake. I'll do this as fast as I can, and then we'll patch him up and hope for the best."

Longarm found his pocket knife and opened his longest and sharpest blade. As a lawman, he'd dug plenty of bullets out of men both good and bad, but this was his first arrowhead, and he hoped it would be his last. After taking a deep breath, Longarm quickly made a pair of incisions out from the edge of the shaft. Andy groaned and thrashed but did not regain consciousness.

"He's *really* bleeding now," Molly said, her face stretched tight with worry.

"I can see that," Longarm whispered, talking to himself, "but I still have to try to pull the arrowhead out again."

But it stuck, so Longarm deepened both incisions. The blood was really flowing as he jammed his fingers into the wound and cut them both on the edge of the iron-tipped arrowhead. Ignoring the pain, he gripped the slippery metal and gritted his teeth as he slowly pried it free.

"There!" he exclaimed, tossing the bloody arrowhead and broken shaft into the brush. "Now let's try to stop the bleeding and bandage him up good and tight."

Redbow crawled over to their side. He had a leather

pouch in his fist. He opened it and then said, "Strong medicine."

"Did you use it on your own leg?" Molly asked skeptically.

"Yes."

"Did he?" she asked, looking to Lucy for confirmation.

"Of course he did! Do you think he'd try to poison that bounty hunter?"

"Sure. He shot him in the back, didn't he?"

"All right," Longarm growled, "that's enough from you two. Redbow, go ahead and use your medicine and then let's bandage Andy and see if he survives until morning."

Redbow took a pinch of powder from his medicine pouch and shoved it deep into Andy's wound, then he clamped his hand over the hole and said what must have been an Indian healing prayer. By then, Molly had a wad of bandaging, and they did the best they could for the bounty hunter.

"He's young," Molly said, swallowing hard. "If he dies, do we even know where he came from?"

Longarm nodded. "His name is Andy Drew and he's from Tucson. He wanted me to let his mother and father know he died and was buried proper."

"I hope he don't end up dead like Hopewell."

"Me, too, although having both Redbow and him wounded makes things far more complicated."

"I see what you mean," Molly said. "Perhaps we'll have to take them both back to the Hopi mesa and then return."

"Yeah," Longarm replied. "I'm going to get some sleep, and I suggest you do the same. We'll sort things out in the morning and make our decision."

And that was how he left it as he stretched out on his bedroll and drifted off to sleep.

In the morning, Andy Drew was awake and in considerable pain. Lucy appeared not to have slept at all and was exhausted, while Molly seemed to be alert.

"Andy," Longarm said, kneeling beside the man, "we have to decide what to do with you."

"I don't think I'm going to die," he said, looking pale but determined. "I made it through the night, but I'm real weak."

"You've lost a great deal of blood. If the wound doesn't poison, I think your chances of recovery are good."

"Me, too, Marshal. But what about that Indian who shot me?" Andy glared at Redbow. "You just going to let him be?"

"I am," Longarm replied. "He's our guide, and we need him. Problem is, he's also wounded."

Longarm had thought Redbow to be sleeping, but the half-breed showed him otherwise when he said, "I'm not staying here or going back to the Hopi. I'm going on with you and finish what I came to do."

"And that is?"

Redbow didn't answer the question but said, "I'll ride one of the extra horses."

"With a bullet hole through your leg?"

"Yes!"

Longarm scowled. "I got a better idea. Why doesn't everyone stay here for a couple of days while I go ahead? If I find the gang, I'll come back for you and then we can decide what our next move should be."

"That makes sense," Lucy agreed.

But Redbow shook his head. "Not to me."

"Listen, dammit, you were the one that jumped the gun on these bounty hunters, and I hold you responsible. When you came, you also agreed to follow my orders, and I'm ordering you to stay right here while I go ahead alone!"

"Maybe I won't follow your orders anymore," Redbow snapped.

"You either follow them or I'll take all the horses. With that hole in your leg, you wouldn't get very far."

Redbow's eyes blazed with fury. "Five days," he managed to say. "Then I come looking for you."

Longarm was in no mood to argue. In five days he could be two hundred miles north in Colorado and either dead or have Yancy Hooker and his men under arrest. "It's a deal."

"Do I have to stay here?" Lucy asked.

"Yes," Longarm replied. "You're the only one healthy enough to forage for wood and keep a high lookout perch. Redbow and Andy need you."

"Then I'll stay."

"I won't," Molly announced. "We've come a long way together, and we'll stay together until this is over."

"Do you understand what you are saying?"

"Yes."

"Well, dammit, you *can't* understand," Longarm blurted, "or you wouldn't be so stubborn!"

"There is no point in arguing, Custis, because I *am* going with you."

Longarm turned to the two bodies. "Guess I'd better bury this pair with rocks," he said. "Andy, were they your friends?"

"No. I met them only a few weeks ago in a Flagstaff saloon. We all needed money, so we pooled what we had and came out here trying to earn the reward."

"I've heard that before," Longarm said. "Do you know if they have any family?"

"The taller one is named Jess. He had a wife once, but she ran off and left him for a traveling preacher."

"And the other?"

"He wasn't too friendly and never said anything about his past."

Longarm looked to the nearest pile of rocks and drawled, "I'm getting damned tired of burying bounty hunters."

"I'll help you," Lucy said. "You grab one leg, and I'll grab the other."

But first, Longarm stooped over and examined their wounds. One had been knifed in the chest, the other shot with a pistol. Both must have died instantly. "Redbow," he said, "you aren't too choosy about how you kill a man, are you."

"What do you mean?"

"Well, you probably shot Andy first as he was running away with your bow, and then you shot this here fella with your six-gun as you charged down into the camp. My guess is the last one got it with that Bowie knife. Am I wrong?"

Redbow said nothing.

"I'm *not* wrong," Longarm said, grabbing the other ankle. "All right, Molly, let's get this over with as quick as we can."

It took them nearly an hour to drag both bodies into the rocks and cover them so that they would not be scavenged. It was a dirty, disagreeable job, but Molly didn't complain, and Longarm had to respect her for that.

"Let's fill the canteens, wash up and get out of here," Longarm said, slapping his hands on his pants.

She didn't seem to be listening. "Death is everywhere in this land. All I see is death."

"Molly," Longarm said, "I sure wish you'd stay here with the others."

"I can't."

"You mean that you *won't*."

"Call it what you want, Custis, but I'm coming with you, so let's not waste any more of our breath. All right?"

"Sure," he said.

A short time later, they were ready to ride. Redbow looked grim, and Andy just looked frail. Longarm stepped into the saddle and said, "We'll be back in five days or less."

"You'd better be," Redbow warned. "Don't even think about trying to jump that gang without me, or you're a dead man."

Longarm didn't bother to reply to that threat. Instead, he turned to Lucy and said, "Take care of them. You've enough food and water. Just keep out of sight and you'll be fine."

"I'll do my best," she replied.

"Let's go," Longarm said, reining his horse around and cutting through the rocks to head north.

Molly was right behind him, and she was heavily armed. He figured he'd need her guns if they stumbled upon any of the Four Corners Gang, and if they did, she'd better be as good at shooting outlaws as she was targets.

Chapter 10

That afternoon Longarm and Lucy were spotted by five mounted Indians who suddenly altered their direction and came galloping forward.

"They're all carrying rifles," Longarm said tight-lipped as he watched the Indians charge across the dry valley they'd been following. "I'm afraid that this could be big trouble."

Lucy's eyes dropped to her shotgun. "Shall we arm ourselves?"

"Yes," Longarm said, unwilling to trust his life to the Indians.

He slipped his Winchester out of his saddle boot while Lucy did the same with her shotgun.

"The last thing we want to do is go to war with this bunch," he told her. "So let's just see if we can have a nice, friendly little conversation and then go our separate ways in peace."

"Do you really think they'll let us go without paying?"

"No, but if the price isn't too high, we'll give in to their request."

"We won't give up our guns, will we?"

"Of course not! Just don't panic and open fire, even if it appears that they mean to kill us."

The five Indians rode scrubby ponies, and although Longarm was uncertain, he guessed that they were Navajo. This was their land, and Longarm had heard that Navajo wore silver and turquoise jewelry like this bunch and were considered to be excellent horsemen.

Longarm raised the Winchester's barrel so that it was pointing slightly over their heads. He also positioned his six-gun for a fast draw before taking a deep, relaxing breath. The five Indians drew their sweaty horses to a halt only a few dozen yards away and, for several tense minutes, did nothing more than glare.

"Hello, there!" Longarm called to break the mounting tension. "We come in peace."

No response.

"I'm a United States Deputy Marshal."

Still no response.

"This isn't starting off too good," Molly whispered. "Have you got any more clever openings?"

"Me Indian agent!"

This caused the Navajo to go into a hurried conference, and soon one detached from the rest and rode forward. He was blocky and dressed in white man's clothes with a blue bandanna tied around his head. His most notable feature was a wicked knife or saber scar that furrowed the crown of his nose.

"You Indian agent?"

"Not exactly, but I've made friends with a few of them," Longarm said, talking fast. "There was Joe Beeker over in Wyoming and Clyde Evans with Mescalero Apache, but they both retired or else got fired, I'm not sure which. And I knew John Alexander, now he was with the Comanche over in the Kansas area."

The Navajo scowled with confusion as Longarm babbled on at Molly. Looking disgusted, he pointed to Molly and barked, "Woman for trade?"

Longarm kept his eyes glued on the horseman and said,

94

"She is my woman and not for trade. Do you have good woman, too?"

The Indian's scowl deepened, and he gave no answer.

"Are you boys Navajo?" Longarm asked with a corn-eating smile.

The horseman dipped his chin.

"That's good, because I'm looking for Yancy Hooker. Where can we find him and his gang?"

"Navajo need guns and horses."

"So do we," Longarm replied with the silly smile pasted on his face.

"Navajo *take* guns and horses!"

"Oh, now come on," Longarm told him. "You know that I can't do without 'em. Molly, what can we give these fine fellas in exchange for the privilege of crossing their land?"

"I have no idea."

"Well," Longarm said, feeling hatred boring into him from the man on horseback, "we need to come up with something."

"Bedrolls and some food. We can't spare the water in our canteens."

"We'll give them a bedroll."

The Navajo must have understood more English than he'd let on because he shouted, "No bedroll. Navajo want guns and horses!"

Longarm allowed the barrel of his rifle to drift down in the general direction of the Indian's face. "We'll give you a good bedroll and a few dollars so that you can buy whiskey or tobacco—but no horses, no guns and no ammunition."

The Navajo jerked his pony around and whipped it back to his friends, who all began to argue. The arguing went on for nearly ten minutes, and then the same Indian returned.

"One gun and one horse or we kill Indian agent and take his woman!"

Longarm knew an ultimatum when he heard one. This fella had reached the end of his patience, and there would be no more silliness or dickering. So he could either cave in and meet the demand, or he could blow a hole in this man's head and then take his chances with the other four. Between himself and Molly, Longarm guessed they might be able to finish off the whole bunch. But what if there were *other* Navajo in the nearby vicinity? Or what if more arrived looking for this bunch and discovered their bullet-riddled bodies?

Longarm didn't like to think what would happen in that case, because he would expect the whole Navajo nation to come down on him and Molly, along with Lucy, Andy and Redbow as well. There would be no hope of escape for any of them. And so, it seemed to Longarm that while they could probably win this battle, they would lose the war and never leave this country alive. If that happened, he'd have failed completely and the Four Corners Gang would continue to rob, raid and rape.

"Molly," he said, not turning from the angry Navajo, "I think he's called our bluff, and we're holding an empty hand."

"You mean you're willing to give them a gun and horse?"

"No choice. Get off your horse and hand him your reins."

"Custis!"

"Do it!"

"Well, dammit, I'm not giving them *my* six-gun!"

"Okay then, draw and kill him, but just remember that there are probably a couple thousand more in these parts, and you'll be passing a death sentence not only on yourself, but on me, Lucy, Redbow and Andy. Are you prepared to take on that kind of responsibility?"

Lucy cussed and dismounted.

"Hand the chief here your reins and then empty your six-gun and give it to him with a smile."

"Why can't he have *your* horse and gun!"

"Because I'm the marshal and you're not even a deputy," Longarm answered. "And because you agreed to do what I told you."

"Well *that* was sure a big mistake!"

"Just do it!"

"Custis, they'll only want more and more. They'll take this as a sign that we are weak, and they won't stop until they have us standing out here unarmed and naked."

"Well, at least I'd enjoy the view."

"Be serious!"

"I am," he told her. "We've got no choice for ourselves or our friends."

Molly emptied her six-gun and shoved it barrel-first to the Navajo.

The Indian did not say "thank you." He did not even look pleased, but instead grunted, "Now bedroll and money."

Longarm untied his own bedroll and gave it to the Indian. Next, he dug into his pockets and slowly counted out eighteen dollars in bills and coins. Handing it to the taciturn Navajo, he smiled and said, "There you go, Chief. This will buy you and your boys plenty at the trading post."

The Navajo folded the goose down across his horse's withers and shoved the money into a leather pouch. He gave Longarm a final look of scorn and then rode back to join his friends. They kicked their ponies into a gallop, whooping and hollering as they led Molly's horse into a cloud of dust.

"Well, Custis, now we're in a *real* mess!"

"At least we're alive. Give me your shotgun and climb up here and we'll ride double until we've put some miles between us and them."

"And just how far do you think they will let us ride before they come back and demand your horse and *all* our weapons?"

"That depends on how greedy they are," he said. "I'm

97

hoping their leader could tell that I won't stand for giving anything more away.''

''Don't bet on it.''

''Molly, I have an idea.''

''Good! It's about time.''

''Why don't we ride along in silence and enjoy the rest of this day?''

She doubled up her fist and punched Longarm in the ribs, but not hard. And despite their extremely sorry circumstances, Longarm couldn't help but smile as he pushed his horse into a ground-eating trot in the opposite direction than the Navajo had just taken. He would try to find a field of rock and hide his tracks, though he doubted that would be possible. If these Navajo were even half as good at tracking as the Apache, the only way that he could lose them would be to take wings. Maybe his best hope was that the Indians would be so anxious to spend their newfound wealth at some distant trading post that they'd let him go free.

Fat damn chance, Longarm thought as he headed toward some rocks and higher ground.

They'd seen no sign of being followed all the rest of that afternoon.

''What do you think?'' Molly asked as they made their camp in a field of boulders and prepared a very small fire to heat beans and pork. ''Do you think they went to spend your money?''

''I don't know. I've never met Navajo before.''

''I doubt they'll stop until they have everything,'' she said.

''You told me that already. Why don't you try to be a little more optimistic?''

''Because only fools are optimistic when the circumstances are this desperate. Here we are somewhere south of the Four Corners, but we have no idea *how* far. We've only got one mount and three canteens of water.''

''Two,'' he corrected, ''I gave one to our horse tonight.''

''Okay, *two* canteens and one happy horse.''

"He's not happy," Longarm assured her. "He could have drunk a whole lot more if it were to be had. But at least he's up to carrying us double tomorrow. After that— well, I don't know."

"Do you think that we ought to just return to Lucy, Redbow and that wounded bounty hunter and call it quits?"

"I've considered that," Longarm admitted, "but we're pretty near the Four Corners, and considering all the hell we've been through, I sure hate to give up now. We might actually find the Hooker hideout tomorrow."

"Then what?" she asked as she stirred the beans and pork onto their tin plates.

Longarm was trying hard to keep up a cheerful front, but it was tough, so he said, "Why don't we just eat, go to bed and let things work themselves out tomorrow? Things can't get any worse."

"You don't mean that." Molly forked down the last of her dinner. "I mean, things could get a damn sight worse."

"Yeah, I guess they could." He studied her closely. "I'll bet you wish that you'd obeyed my orders and turned back when we first met."

"Listen, Custis, I've a mission just the same as you and Redbow and Lucy. And all of us want the same thing—to stop the Four Corners Gang. To put an end to their reign of terror over this part of the country once and for all."

"Well," Longarm mused as he finished his coffee and beans and went to his bedroll, "we'll just do our damnedest to make sure that happens. But if we fail, we can at least say that we gave it a good try."

"Where am I supposed to sleep?"

"Beside me."

"Oh?"

"Don't worry, I don't bite."

"Hilda told me that, but she also mentioned that you are a very lusty man."

"Molly, given our situation, you *have* to be kidding."

"Yeah," she yawned, "I guess we are sort of worn a bit too thin to worry about that sort of thing."

"Of course we are. Now kick some dirt on the fire and let's go to sleep."

"All right. Maybe you'll even come up with a plan by morning."

"I probably will. As a matter of fact, a lot of my best ideas come while I'm in bed."

"So I've heard."

He rolled over to stare at her in the moonlight. "And exactly what is *that* supposed to mean?"

"Nothing."

"Sure it did."

"Hilda told me that you told her you knew a dozen ways to make love to a woman."

"No!"

"Yes. And she said that you showed her every one of them."

Longarm barked a laugh of derision. "Did Hilda also admit that she knew a couple I hadn't even thought of?"

"No, but that wouldn't surprise me. That woman sure loves men."

"Yep, and she needs about three of them a night to keep her satisfied. I've never seen a woman with such a lusty appetite."

"Wore you out, huh?"

"Pretty near."

"I haven't made love for a long, long time," Molly sadly informed him. "You see, after what the Four Corners Gang forced me to do, I can't even bear the idea of making love with a man."

"I'm sorry," he said, meaning it.

"It was worse than any nightmare," she told him, her eyes suddenly brimming with tears. "For a long time after it happened, I thought about killing myself."

Longarm leaned up on one elbow. "Why?"

"I felt so dirty! I bathed a hundred times and scrubbed

myself raw where they'd been, but it didn't help.''

"I hope that you'll get past that feeling soon," Longarm told her.

"I wonder if I ever will."

Longarm was tired, but he had an idea. "Molly, perhaps you should . . . aw, never mind. Let's get some sleep."

"What were you going to suggest?"

"Nothing."

"I want to know."

Longarm frowned. "When a cowboy gets thrown and hurt, he has to get back in the saddle and ride soon or he's no good anymore. When a man gets whipped, if he becomes afraid to stand up for his rights, he's no good to himself or anyone else anymore. What I'm saying, Molly, is that I've learned you have to face your fears—just meet them head on."

"That's easier said than done."

"Of course it is, but they usually aren't nearly as bad as they've grown to be in your mind."

"What happened when those animals raped me certainly wasn't just 'in my mind,' Custis! It was real and it *was* horrible."

"I wasn't trying to tell you different."

"Then what were you trying to tell me?"

"Only that you will make love again because you are brave and a healthy woman who has a lot of love to offer. And when it happens, you'll probably be healed."

The bitterness left her voice, and she studied Longarm closely. "Do you really think it will be that simple?"

"No," he confessed, "but this will pass, and I think I know you well enough to predict that you'll come out of it whole again."

"Custis?"

"Yes?"

"Would *you* make love to me?"

"Huh?"

"I want you to make love to me, but do it gentle. I need

some sweet and gentle loving if I'm going to get past this sickness I have inside.''

"Molly, if you need someone real gentle, wait and find a nice fella. Maybe a fella who dresses good, bathes every day and goes to take his mother to church every Sunday.''

"Hilda says you can be gentle.''

He swallowed. "Now, and out here in the dirt?''

"Yes. I'm scared, and if my worst nightmare happens when we come upon the gang, maybe I'll be able to remember us tonight and not go crazy.''

He put his arms around her. "Molly, I don't think you—''

But Longarm didn't finish because she kissed his lips. Up to that very moment, Longarm hadn't been thinking about anything except the Four Corners Gang and those five Navajo. But her kiss was eager, and it sort of got his mind on a new, more pleasant track. So he kissed her back, and she unbuttoned his shirt and ran her fingers lightly over the hair on his chest.

"Scared?'' he teased.

"Don't say a word. Just do it gentle.''

Molly unbuttoned her shirt and drew it back from her shoulders so that he could admire her breasts. Longarm cupped them like honey melons and began to lick and suck on them until the woman squirmed with pleasure.

"How are you doing?'' he asked.

"Good, so far!''

"I thought so.''

He worked Molly's nipples into hard little buttons and then removed her pants and began to run his hand up and down her silken thighs until she was digging at his pants and breathing as if she'd run uphill a couple of miles. Longarm ran his tongue slowly down between her breasts until he reached her belly.

"Oh my!'' she panted. "This isn't going to be a bit difficult!''

"You mean you're already cured?''

102

"Not yet. Don't stop!"

"I wasn't planning to," Longarm promised as he raised his hips and then teased her with the end of his throbbing rod.

Molly's hips surged to greet him, but Longarm declined her, and she cried, "Custis, you're driving me insane!"

"Are you very sure?"

"Of course!" she gasped, digging her fingernails into his buttocks and impaling herself with a cry of pleasure.

"All right," he promised, "slow; we'll take our time and go slow and easy."

"Yes, yes! But not . . . Oh please! Gentle but not *too* easy!"

Longarm was especially gentle and took a long time working Molly into a fever pitch. Then he toyed with her until she writhed and begged for satisfaction. By now, Molly was humping and huffing, and her heels were locked behind Longarm's knees as she moaned and shuddered. "Do it! Do it, Custis!"

"My extreme pleasure!" he growled as his slick rod plowed deep and his hips stiffened to unleash a torrent of his seed. Longarm had always possessed a great reservoir, and women marveled at how long it took him to empty his sack. Again and again he roared as he filled Molly until they both suddenly went limp.

"Oh my," she gasped, fighting for breath. "I can't believe how that washed away my nightmare!"

He started to climb off her, but Molly hugged him with all her might. "Thank you. Thank you!"

"My pleasure and privilege," he said, meaning it.

After a while, he rolled off and they fell asleep. Once in the night, Longarm awakened and thought he heard a sound, but then Molly was climbing on top of him and working his manhood into arousal, so he did his very best to ensure that her nightmare never returned. Sleep came again and lasted until the sun came up through the rocks near midmorning.

"Custis!"

"Can't it wait until after—"

"No," Molly cried. "Our horse is gone!"

Longarm jumped up and looked all around. Not only was his horse gone, but so was his saddle, canteens, the shotgun and his Winchester.

"Dammit!" he cried. "We've been cleaned out by those Navajo!"

"We're dead," Molly wailed. "We should have died last night making love."

Longarm reached for his pants, grateful that he at least had his boots, revolver, knife and the derringer.

"Custis, what are we going to do!"

"Follow their tracks and get everything back from those thieving Navajo," he vowed. "And I mean *everything*!"

"Yes," Molly said, trying hard not to cry. "We can't let them get away with this."

Longarm gave the woman a hug and even managed to dredge up a smile. "Molly," he said, "no matter what else happens, I want to say you've got sand."

"That's good, huh?"

"In a bad fix like this, it counts for most everything," Longarm told her. "Now let's eat whatever grub we have, gather up our canteens and start after them thievin' Navajo. I got a hunch they'll expect us to just give up and head back south."

"What about our bedroll?"

"Leave it," he decided, "we aren't going to be using it again for a while, if ever."

Molly built a fire, made coffee and warmed up some more beans while Longarm went to inspect the tracks left by the Navajo horse thieves. Yep, it was the same bunch that they'd encountered yesterday.

"Custis," she said when he came back to their camp to wolf down some breakfast, "do you really think we can catch those Indians and reclaim our horses and weapons?"

"Sure I do," he said, "because it's the only thing we can do."

She squeezed his hand. "I don't know if you're just saying that to make me feel better or not, but it's working."

"We'll get out of this and accomplish what we started out to do, Molly. Just keep your chin up and everything will work out fine."

"I believe in you, Custis."

He looked away suddenly, trying to hide both his fear and his emotion. Longarm felt his throat tighten painfully because it was one thing to put your own life on the line and maybe lose it, but quite another to jeopardize a brave and wonderful woman like Molly.

Chapter 11

"Custis, I've got heel blisters on both feet, and I'm thirsty, hot and tired!"

"Well, I'm not skip-tee-doo-dahin' it up this mountainside myself!" he snapped in reply.

"Can't we rest just a few minutes and have a sip of water?"

"No."

"Dammit, why not?"

Longarm was limping and fresh out of patience because Molly had been badgering him all afternoon to stop and rest and each time he'd had to give her the same reply. "Because these hoof prints we're following aren't getting any fresher."

It had been a long, long day, and Custis's own feet were sprouting blisters, but he wasn't lying about the hoof prints they followed not growing any fresher. If anything, the Navajo horse thieves were extending the distance between them, and that was very bad news. To Longarm's way of thinking, their only chance was to overtake the Navajo, recapture their weapons and horses and then forge on toward Four Corners and try to catch the Hooker bunch by surprise.

"It's almost sundown," Molly panted, pushing up to

grab his arm and haul him around so that she could look him in the face. "Surely those Indians sleep at night."

"I don't know if they sleep, but *we* won't."

"Oh!" she wailed. "I'm dead on my feet."

Longarm expelled a deep breath, wrapped his arms around her and smoothed her hair. "Listen, honey," he said wearily. "If our luck changes, the Navajo will have stopped by now for the night and we'll be able to overtake and catch them by surprise while they are sleeping. It has to be tonight because we won't have the strength to push on for another day at this pace."

"What if the Indians *don't* make camp?"

"Then we keep going because our only hope is to pass out of Indian country and reach Colorado. Once there, we can get help and horses. We'll provision ourselves and return to rescue Lucy, Redbow and Andy Drew. They're counting on us, and we can't fail them . . . or ourselves."

"I know," she rasped, "it's just that I'm so thirsty that my tongue is swelling up in my mouth, and I'm getting dizzy."

Longarm gazed at the sun, which would be setting in about a half hour. "All right," he agreed, leading Molly over to the shade of a tree. "Let's have a couple swallows and rest until the sun goes down. After that, there ought to be enough moonlight to follow the tracks."

"Thank you!"

Longarm smoothed a place on the ground for Molly and then for himself. "Close your eyes and nap a few minutes."

"What about you?"

"I don't dare," he told her. "If I closed my eyes, neither one of us might wake up until tomorrow morning, and we'd be in one hell of a bad fix."

"If you won't sleep, then I won't."

"Don't be ridiculous. Close your eyes."

Longarm couldn't have counted to ten in the time it took Molly Murphy to fall asleep. He studied her face in the glow of sunset and saw that it was streaked with lines where sweat and dust had joined. Her eyes and cheeks appeared sunken and, even though she wore a man's hat, Molly's pretty face was burnt from the sun, and her hair was caked with dirt. Longarm picked a piece of twig out of it and silently swore in frustration. Molly was giving it all she had, but her strength could not match his, and she was beginning to fail.

We've just got to overtake those Indians tonight or I'm going to have to leave her with our water and strike out fast for help. She won't last another full day.

The idea of leaving Molly alone in this harsh wilderness was depressing, so Longarm dwelled on it no more but instead tried to focus his mind on how and what he would do when they caught up with the sleeping Navajo. He had a gun and a cartridge belt of bullets. He also had a derringer and a knife.

You can't afford to kill them or you'll bring the whole Navajo nation down on your heads. You have to steal their horses and leave them stranded and far behind. But that won't be easy.

The sun slipped into the western horizon, and Longarm delayed waking Molly up for another half hour. When he did wake her up, she was sleeping so soundly that he had to almost carry her the first mile before she completely awakened.

"I was dreaming," she told him as they plodded up another long grade.

"About what?"

"About us making love." Molly licked her cracked and bleeding lips. "It was the first nice dream I've had in a good long while."

"I'm glad," he said, taking her hand and leading her over a rough patch of ground. When they passed beyond it, Longarm decided to just keep holding her hand.

"If we live through this, what will you do?" she asked.

"I'll go back to Flagstaff, wire my boss Billy Vail that I've managed to put a stop to the Four Corners Gang, and then I'm just going to stay in town and relax.''

"Hilda will be real happy about that.''

"Damn,'' he muttered, "I'd forgotten Hilda. In the run-down condition I'm in, I sure won't be up to meeting her sexual expectations. Maybe I won't stay in Flagstaff.''

"You'll just leave Arizona?''

"I'm not sure. But it's certain that if I go back to Denver I'll immediately be put on another assignment.''

"Then don't go back so soon.''

"Molly, do you know anything about Prescott? Someone once told me that it is a good, relaxing town.''

"It is,'' Molly replied. "I happen to know some people there. Maybe I'll come along with you.''

She said it kind of off-handedly, but when Longarm glanced at Molly, she was watching him closely to judge his reaction. "I'd like that very much. Are there some good places we could eat?''

"Wonderful places,'' she said. "It's not as high as Flagstaff, but not desert country, and the air will be cool and fresh.''

"Then that's what we'll do,'' he decided as if they were on their way to church instead of trying to jump a bunch of Indians. "Either that, or we'll head on over to Durango and take it easy for a few weeks.''

"Either way is fine with me, Custis.'' She squeezed his hand, and when he glanced down at her face, Molly was smiling.

They walked the better part of the night before they smelled smoke and knew that they had at last overtaken the Navajo.

"I guess this is our moment of truth, huh?'' she whispered as they crept forward, no longer feeling the pain of their many blisters.

"It is,'' he said, stopping short and trying to judge the layout of the camp. The Indians had corralled their horses in a deep, narrow draw and blocked its only exit with ropes. Unfortunately, the draw opened into their camp and, at first glance, it appeared that there was no way that they could steal the horses without waking the Indians.

"Custis, what are we going to do!"

"I'm thinking."

"We'll never untie those ropes without waking the Indians. And maybe there is a sentry sneaking up on us right now!"

"Shhh!" Longarm urged.

He removed his Ingersol pocket watch, whose chain was soldered to the twin-barreled .44 caliber derringer, and then handed it to her. "Don't lose this."

Molly had seen it before but said, "Custis, I've never fired a derringer."

"It's no different than firing a revolver, except that you can't hit anything beyond about twenty feet."

"Well, then. . . ."

"Trust me," Longarm told her. "When all hell breaks loose, these Navajo will be so busy jumping and running for cover that they won't know you can't possibly hit them except by accident. So just fire it like a regular gun."

"How about some extra bullets?"

He gave her a handful from his cartridge belt and then told her exactly what they had to do next.

Molly had reached the corral, and Longarm could see her using his knife to cut the ropes. The Indian ponies were alert, but she'd moved slowly, so they were not milling or alarmed. Longarm, meanwhile, had sneaked right into the Indians' camp and collected every pistol he could find and tied them all up in a bundle that he'd slung over his shoulder. No doubt there were some he'd missed but, hopefully, not many. He sure wished he could have done the same with the rifles, but it was physical impossibility, so he hid them off a ways so that the Indians couldn't use them in a hurry.

The moon was both a blessing and a curse. On the one hand it allowed him to see Molly and her to see him, but on the other hand it would also show the Navajo that they were up against only the same two people whose horses they had already stolen. That meant that they would not be intimidated and would choose to fight.

Well, Longarm thought, *if all goes as planned, by the time they realize what is up, we'll be on their horses and out of firing range.*

He signaled for Molly to mount her horse and then, as Longarm took his stand at the opposite end of the camp, he made a slashing motion with his arm that could not be missed. On cue, Molly fired the derringer and sent the horses charging out of their corral directly over the sleeping figures.

Everything happened almost too fast to comprehend. The horses trampled some of the sleeping Indians, but probably jumped over most of them because they naturally did not like to step on anything other than solid ground. Longarm saw one Navajo leap to his feet and scream, but he was bowled over by a stampeding horse. Other Navajo could be heard wailing or shouting, but by then Molly was driving through the camp and pulling her excited mount up for Longarm.

"Nice work!" he shouted, swinging onto the animal and gripping her tightly around the waist. "Now let's drive them north just as far as we can before they decide to scatter!"

"We really did it!"

"So far, so good," Longarm shouted as her flying hair whipped his cheeks. "You were wonderful!"

"So were you!"

They thundered across the moonlit valley, eating the dust of the Navajo ponies and loving it. Longarm guessed that they ran at least five miles before the ponies began to tire. His own horse was one of the first to quit, and he wasted no time catching it to ride bareback. Thanks to Molly's foresight, it was bridled.

"Let's give them a breather," Longarm called, as he reined up and then dismounted.

"I can't believe we did it," Molly exclaimed, twisting around and gazing back across the miles they'd run. "I never thought we'd pull it off without bloodshed."

"Well, we did, and now they'll be the ones that will be walking and trying hard to overtake us."

Molly's exuberant smile faded. "I hadn't thought of that."

"It's a good thing their ponies are gentle and still together. I won't stop looking back until we've driven them another twenty miles or more."

"Me neither," she said.

Longarm lit a cigar and enjoyed a quiet smoke while Molly sat down and watched their back trail.

"See anything?"

"Of course not," she answered. "Just the dust hanging behind us, which is lovely the way it glows in the moonlight. Like a golden cloud."

He smiled. "Maybe you should have been a poet."

"No," Molly said, "though I love to read poetry. I'd rather be . . ."

"What?"

"I don't know. I used to want nothing more than to be a rancher's wife and raise four or five healthy children. Now, I'm not so sure."

"Why?"

Molly shrugged. "Having gone through so much, I kind of think I might want to have a bit more excitement in my life."

He laughed. "Haven't you had enough danger to last a lifetime?"

"Yes, but right now I feel so . . . exhilarated by what we've just accomplished that I sort of feel that I'd like more." She studied him. "Is that why you've been a marshal for so many years and hate the idea of getting promoted to a desk job like your boss?"

112

"I suppose so," Longarm replied. "When I'm out in the field I bitch and moan about the hardships and sometimes take chances I shouldn't. I'm usually tired and dirty and yearning for my bed in Denver and the comforts of that city. But . . ."

"But then you start to missing it pretty quick. Right?"

"Right," he told her. "Maybe someday the excitement or whatever it is that keeps me moving will grow old just as I will grow old. They say that age makes a man timid and afraid."

"Not you, Custis. If you live to be eighty—which I doubt—you'll still be an adventuring old man."

He laughed. "Since neither of us expects me to live that long, I don't think I have to fret about that happening. But I *have* known old men that never lost their love of excitement and adventure. Some were mountain men that kept going back to the high, wild country until they died or got too blind or feeble. Others have been ranchers, frontiersmen and explorers. Fellas that just had to always see what was on the other side of the mountain."

"I'll bet you'll be that way until you die."

"Maybe." Longarm rubbed out his half-smoked cigar on his boot heel. "I think we'd best be moving again. The sun will be up in about an hour."

"I know. I should be exhausted. I *was* exhausted only a short time ago, but I'm not anymore."

"Me neither. Let me give you a hand up on your horse. By the way, how'd you do it without stirrups?"

"I really don't know," she confessed. "I was so excited when I fired that derringer and started driving horses that I just jumped up as easy as you please."

"That happens sometimes," Longarm said with a nod. "You get real excited, and you can do remarkable things that you couldn't imagine doing any other time."

"Well, this isn't one of those times, and I would appreciate a little help up now."

Longarm got her mounted and then jumped onto his own

horse, and they continued north, pushing the Navajo ponies. Daybreak found them at least fifteen miles north of the Navajo camp and moving at a steady pace.

"We've got to find water by noon," Longarm told Molly. "These horses can't keep going."

"I know, but I have a feeling we'll find it!"

"You do?"

"Sure. Our luck has finally changed for the better!"

"I believe it has," he told her, untying the bundle he'd taken from the Indian camp. "I even managed to recover your six-gun."

"No holster?"

"Molly, sometimes you can't have everything," he said.

"I know," she replied, looking at him with a trace of sadness. "I'll never be able to have you for long."

He had nothing to say to that, so they continued to drive the ponies and eat their dust. Longarm saw a storm front up to the north and hoped that it would rain.

"Do you have any idea how far we are from Four Corners?"

"Not far."

"And then?"

"I'll think of something," he told her with a wink.

"Yeah," she said, dredging up a tired smile. "I've heard that one before."

After that, they rode apart and were kept busy herding because the ponies kept wanting to peel off from the bunch and graze.

"Water," Longarm whispered, watching as Molly tried to prevent the Indian ponies from breaking off and changing directions toward the east.

"Custis, I can't stop them!"

He rode hard to help, and then it hit him that the Indian ponies probably knew exactly where to find the nearest water hole. "Let 'em run!" he shouted.

"What!"

"Let 'em run! They think they're headed for water!"

114

"But what if that also happens to be where we find a big Navajo Indian village or something!"

"Then *that's* when I'll figure out what to do next!"

Molly shook her head but slowed her horse to wait for him. They exchanged glances and kept riding after the galloping ponies.

Won't be long now, Longarm thought as they sailed across the brush and rocks trying hard to keep up with the thirst-crazed band of Indian ponies.

Chapter 12

The Navajo ponies streamed through a narrow pass with Longarm and Molly right on their heels.

"Holy cow!" Molly cried, pulling up hard on her reins. "More Indians!"

Longarm saw the Navajo sheep camp located beside a stream with grass and trees. "Molly, we need their water!"

The Navajo village wasn't very large, and, as they drew closer, Longarm supposed that it was more of a summer grazing camp than a permanent settlement. At the sight of the stampeding ponies and onrushing riders, Navajo women and children began to scream and ran to hide. Five or six men, some of them quite old, grabbed their weapons and hurried forward as if they expected to be attacked.

"Hold up!" Longarm shouted, drawing his horse to a stop.

But Molly's animal could not be controlled, and she went flying after the stampeding ponies past the armed men and through the camp. She didn't come to a stop until her horse slid down a shallow embankment and began to suck great gulps of water from the stream.

The Navajo did not know what to think of this, and if Molly hadn't yanked off her hat to show them her long hair, someone might have opened fire. Longarm raised his hand in a sign of peace and, when the Indians lowered their weapons, rode forward.

"United States Marshal Long," he shouted, digging out his badge and displaying it to everyone. "Friend of Navajo."

That wasn't exactly true, but Longarm *wanted* to be friends.

The men gestured that he was to dismount and come forward. Meanwhile, Molly had jumped off her horse into a stream and was now lying face down gulping water as fast as she could swallow.

It was clear to Longarm that these were simple shepherds who had no evil intentions. So he smiled and found one of the men who spoke broken English and explained that they needed food, saddles and canteens to carry water. In return, they would give the Navajo all the horses except those that they rode.

"We *have* to tell them where we got those Indian ponies," Molly insisted. "Otherwise, we are putting these shepherds in a bad spot."

"I was coming to that," Longarm replied. He studied the Navajo sheep men one by one and finally announced, "These are Navajo ponies. Their riders will be here in a day."

The man he specifically addressed frowned and led his friends over to the stream where they inspected the ponies. After a lengthy conversation, they returned to Longarm and agreed to his terms.

"Good!" Longarm said with relief. He untied the heavy bundle he carried slung over his shoulder, and the Navajo crowded around to stare at the pistols. Longarm counted seven. "I would like to trade these for two good rifles."

"They belong to same Navajo?"

"That's right."

"Hmmm."

Once again the Indians went off to confer. Two hours passed, during which Longarm napped and their horses devoured the nourishing meadow grass. Finally, the Indians returned and agreed to his terms. In exchange for the seven pistols, Longarm received a couple of old seven-shot Spencer rifles, which he immediately test fired and found to be accurate. A Spencer was light enough for Molly to handle and could be emptied in less than fifteen seconds. Its only real drawback was that it lacked the stopping power of a Winchester and had the reputation of being prone to jamming and misfires. Still, these rifles would be a big advantage over pistols in this wide-open country.

"You need to hide those pistols and ponies before the five men we took them from come to this sheep camp," Longarm warned. "I do not want you to be punished."

"No punish. Navajo steal horses then they are *his* horses. Navajo lose horses . . ."

The Indian shrugged to indicate that stealing and having your horses stolen was expected even between his people. He also pointed to the hills and, for the first time, Longarm saw other shepherds pushing their flocks down toward the camp where they would be held in safety during the night. These new arrivals meant that this camp was strong enough to stand up to the five pursuers.

Longarm gathered his watered and grass-fed horses and led them back to the camp where the trade saddles waited. He'd never ridden an Indian saddle, but it wasn't much different in design from the McClellan saddle used all across the West by the United States Cavalry. It was light, and the wooden tree was wrapped with rawhide, which was extremely hard and uncomfortable. These saddles used ropes instead of leathers to connect with the stirrups. No saddle horn. No cantle or pommel to speak of, but they offered a heck of a lot more support than riding bareback, so Longarm wasn't complaining.

"I am after the Four Corners Gang," he said while he cinched the saddles down tight. "They are led by a man named Yancy Hooker. Do you know him and his brothers?"

"Bad men. They kill you slow."

"Not if we get the drop on them first."

The Navajo sheep man was not impressed and raised his hand to point east. "Ride that way to Fort Wingate and blue coats."

"I can't do that."

He looked at Molly, and Longarm knew he was thinking that this marshal was a fool and that soon he and his woman would both be feeding vultures.

"I've got a sack of dried mutton and another of corn meal," Molly announced as she returned, surrounded by a crowd of women and children. "Did you get ammunition for the rifles?"

"As much as I could." Longarm finished saddling the second horse. "This is going to feel better than riding bareback, but not much."

"I just hope these people aren't punished by those who follow us."

One of the sheep men overheard this and said, "Navajo steal from Navajo, no trouble. Navajo steal from whites or other Indian peoples, much trouble. Navajo maybe sell or trade other ponies to Navajo."

"I understand," Longarm said, as he climbed into the saddle and was handed the Spencer rifle. What this man had just told him was that when the five men arrived, they would be traded fresh horses and would probably continue the pursuit. That meant that there was no time to waste. "Good luck!"

Molly waved as they left the camp. They passed slowly through the flock of sheep, not wanting to scatter and possibly injure them. But once clear of the flock, Longarm pushed his horse into a lope that he would try to hold for at least five miles.

"We made it!" Molly shouted, riding beside him with a big grin on her face. "They were so nice! I would have enjoying staying there for a few days and getting to know them better."

"Too bad," he said. "But we're not out of danger yet."

"Why?"

"Because they will trade or sell the men who pursue us more horses."

"Oh," Molly said. "So we've got trouble behind and even more trouble ahead."

"That's right."

"Are you sure we shouldn't go to Fort Wingate and get reinforcements?"

"I'll take you there, but the Army won't come this far, and I'm sure they wouldn't help us arrest the gang. That's not their role."

"Then what is their role?"

"You'd have to ask them," Longarm shouted. "Used to be fighting Indians and protecting settlers and passengers. Now . . . well, I don't know for sure."

That night they were fortunate enough to intercept another stream. The country was still arid, but there were tall mountains to the east and some grassland. Longarm and Molly tried to keep an all-night vigil, for they did not want anyone to steal their horses again. But they fell asleep soon after midnight and didn't awaken until dawn.

Longarm sat up with a start of alarm, the Spencer still gripped in his hands. But their horses were still hobbled and grazing nearby along with a buck and two does. Taking careful aim, Longarm shot the buck through the shoulders, and it died instantly. The horses bolted and would have run away in fright, but he caught and settled them.

Molly, still half-asleep was furious. "Did you have to wake us up like that!"

"I did if you want to have some fresh venison. Those deer would have vanished into the trees in another few minutes. Do you know how to butcher one?"

"No."

"Sure you do," he said, grabbing the three-point buck and dragging it over to their camp. "But I'll do the honors if you gather some firewood and do the roasting.''

"You got a deal," she told him.

In less than an hour, they were enjoying the fresh venison and turning strips over the fire to pack away with the mutton and corn meal.

"At least we're not in danger of starving anymore," Longarm said as he got up and walked over to the stream to wash and drink deeply before they struck out again.

"Custis, don't you have any idea how much farther it is to the Four Corners?"

"Less than fifty miles, or I'm badly mistaken. Could be as little as ten or twenty. Either way, we're close enough to run into the gang today."

"In a way, I'll be glad when we finally do. I'm tired of worrying and wondering what will happen."

"I know what you mean," he told her. "I feel the same way myself."

Molly seemed to tarry while he caught up and saddled their horses. And when he asked her why, she said, "I'm just tired of chasing and being chased. I'd like to stay here and rest for a few days. If there wasn't any chance of us being followed, would you enjoy that, too?"

"I would," he said. "I'd like it even better if I had some whiskey and fresh cigars, but we'd get by fine."

"We'd do better than 'fine,' " she said. "We'd make love all the time, and it would be wonderful."

He had to chuckle. "Sounds like you've sort of got things right in your mind again."

"You mean about making love with you?"

"Or men in general."

Her smile died, and she wrapped her arms tight around his waist, laying her head against his chest. "It's just you I want, Custis. No other man. Not ever."

Longarm wanted to tell her that this attitude would also change. That he'd leave her in time, when she was safe and strong and confident again. And then Molly would find a man who wanted marriage, and she'd have children and

121

live a good, long life. But looking down into her eyes right now, he decided that she didn't want to hear any of that, so he just kissed the top of her head and hugged her right back.

They stood like that for quite some time and, finally, he said, "Molly, we've got to be leaving."

"Yeah, I know. I'll pack up the rest of our things and be ready in a few minutes."

Longarm watched her go back to the camp. She was a very fine and handsome woman. Her presence had meant a lot to him, and they'd done well together so far. But he couldn't help but worry about what would happen next.

He didn't have long to wait. Before the sun was directly overhead, his horse threw a shoe and went lame.

"Rock bruise," he told her, unable to hide his disgust.

"What are we going to do now?"

"We'll ride yours double, and I'll lead mine."

Molly twisted around and stared south. "We won't be able to make much time."

"I know that."

"Then what—"

"Molly," he said, "let's just do this and keep moving."

"All right," she said, "but now I really think we ought to head for Fort Wingate."

"What about all that talk you made concerning how you had to settle the score with the Hooker men?"

She swallowed hard. "To be honest, I'd kind of forgotten how much hate I had inside. I credit you for that, Custis."

Longarm didn't have a response, so he swung up behind her and they just kept on moving.

Chapter 13

Redbow had walked a little farther each day, starting with the day when Longarm and Molly had left him behind. His wound still pained him, but pain was something that he had learned to master at a very young age.

"I am going north to find the Marshal and that woman," he announced on the fifth day when Longarm had not returned. "I no longer have need of a horse."

"You'll never catch Marshal Long and Molly walking!" Andy Drew protested. "Man, that's rough country up there, and you might run into trouble."

Redbow did not bother to respond, for he considered the young bounty hunter unworthy of debate. He held the woman named Lucy in only slightly higher regard, but he knew of her suffering at the hands of the Four Corners Gang and admired the spirit inside her that gave her the strength to seek revenge.

"Andy is right," Lucy said. "You ought to stay here with us and wait."

"Five days have passed. I will wait no longer." Redbow thought they were both more worried about their own safety than his. However, he chose not to say this and instead told them, "You keep good watch."

"What about our weapons?" Andy demanded. "I can't

protect Lucy with my bare hands if you take 'em.''

Redbow did not think this man was capable of protecting the woman, even with many rifles. "I take only my knife, pistols, bow and arrows. And one canteen."

"You'll never make it," Lucy told him. "Not on foot. If that bullet wound opens up again, you'll lie down and bleed to death in an hour or two. Vultures might pick your bones before we could find you."

Redbow had no use for any more words, so he filled his canteen, made a small pack for food and gathered his long bow and quiver. "You stay here. Maybe live. Maybe die."

"Well, that sure ain't much in the way of encouragement!" Andy snapped. "I guess I'll have to do the protectin' if Indians or outlaws find us."

Lucy came over to Redbow and said, "If you make it out, you'll try to send help for us, won't you?"

Redbow wanted to offer this woman some comfort because he had grown to respect her. But comforting words had never been part of his vocabulary, so he simply dipped his chin, turned on his heel and limped away.

"You're a fool!" Andy shouted. "The Marshal said to wait here for him to come back!"

Redbow did not listen but instead kept walking. He was not sure how many miles he could travel this first day. Maybe no more than five, but perhaps as many as ten. Certainly not anything like what he could have done had he not been shot. But however far he went, it would be closer to the men he intended to kill. If it also turned out that he could help Molly Murphy and the marshal, that was fine. But if not, too bad.

As he walked along, he thought of his past and how it had always seemed that he had been all alone and fighting everyone and everything. His father had been a huge, hard-drinking Army sergeant. Redbow remembered that he had been called a Pollock, but that meant nothing. His mother had been Comanche, and she had lived with her brutish husband at a fort in Texas washing clothes and cooking for the officers and their wives to earn extra money. But when Redbow was born, she became very sick and had never completely recovered. All this he had been told later by a friend of his father, another sergeant named Mike Rafferty. His father had been killed by the Apache while out on patrol, and Sergeant Rafferty had persuaded missionaries to send Redbow to an Indian school in Oklahoma. But most of the children there had been full-blooded Choctaw, Cherokee, Chickasaw and other tribes, so he made no friends, but many enemies. He was named Redbow there because he had used a broken red table leg to carve a bow and arrows over a span of two years and then had shot one of his most relentless tormentors in the buttocks. For this act, he was whipped so severely that he still bore a latticework of scars across his own back and buttocks.

During his early years, Redbow had always been losing fights with boys older than himself. He had more fist and whip scars on his body than he could count, but by the time he was fifteen (and already six-foot-two), he had learned to beat men. After that, the school sent him packing, but not before he'd learned to read and write. Redbow had come to Arizona because of Sergeant Rafferty. He'd intended to whip him, too, for sending him to the hated Indian school, but the man had died the year before in Silver City, New Mexico, of the French disease so common among frontier soldiers.

Redbow was an outcast and a drifter and worked wherever the wages were too low or the work too hard and dangerous for anyone but a half-breed, a black man or a Mexican. He learned hard lessons everywhere he lived and fought men with increasing viciousness and skill until he had killed a Flagstaff muleskinner. Not that it hadn't been a fair fight, because he had not been the one who chose to humiliate and insult the other. But Redbow learned that cruel words were weapons, too, and when they were used against him, he knew an instant and murderous rage that was not satisfied until the man who had used words against

125

him was bloodied and battered senseless. The giant mule-skinner had been acclaimed the toughest brawler in all of Arizona Territory and had never been beaten. In the end, when Redbow had broken his face, his fists and even his arms, he had still refused to be beaten and so had died cursing Redbow.

Redbow felt no guilt or regret, but when a lynch mob threatened to burst him out of jail and stretch his neck, the worried marshal turned him free. Redbow fled into the only place where a mob would not follow—into the Indian country.

The Four Corners Gang caught and dragged him with their ropes through the brush, rocks and cactus. They tied his hands over his head and practiced stripping even more of his flesh away with bullwhips. And when he could no longer speak, curse or even twitch, Yancy Hooker ordered him staked naked to the sun and left him to cook and scream until the vultures pecked out his eyes and shredded his thirst-swollen tongue.

Had it not been for the Hopi, Redbow would have died badly. He should have died. Had it not been for Hopi spirits, medicines, prayers and kindness, his bones would have been bleached and scattered while his tortured spirit roamed the winds, screaming silently for revenge.

Redbow limped to the next water hole and slept most of the evening. He left that place with no sign of his passing and continued with nothing except his weapons and a canteen. He thought of nothing except of killing Yancy Hooker and the men who had staked him naked in the sun to die. Redbow hoped to save the marshal and the woman, for they were brave and kind. But that was not his mission, and their lives did not greatly matter. This wasn't about white man's justice, it was about revenge, exactly the way Redbow wanted it to be. If he was killed, as seemed likely since his enemies were many and his resources to slay them few, it was his rightful destiny. Only he must not fall into their hands again and suffer their tortures. No, he must die fighting. Being captured, stripped, humiliated, degraded and tortured was Redbow's only consuming fear.

Days later, he found the camp where the marshal and the woman had allowed the Navajo to steal their horses. Redbow also expected to find their bodies, but instead discovered another camp by a stream where a careful examination of tracks told him that the whites had been successful in recapturing not only their horses, but also five more Navajo ponies.

Redbow almost grinned.

His stamina returning and his leg growing stronger, Redbow began to run a little each day, always wrapping his wound tightly so that the healing did not tear open and his blood pour out.

He ran most of the way to the Navajo sheepherders' camp; his presence seemed to unnerve them, so he did not stay, except long enough to learn that the five Navajo had gotten new ponies and continued after the marshal and his white woman. They had, of course, been shamed in the eyes of their own people. Redbow understood the force of shame. He had been born in a state of shame, and it had only been when shame had evolved into hatred and fury that he became truly alive. Had he not been tortured, left to die and then saved by the Hopi, he would not now feel the need to avenge himself against the evil that lived in men like Yancy Hooker, his brothers and their hated outlaw band.

What would happen if he survived and satisfied his consuming revenge? Redbow thought he would only discover the answer to this question in a ceremonial kiva among the spiritual leaders of the Hopi. Beyond that, he thought of nothing.

Nothing at all.

Run you son of a drunken Pollock sergeant, you half-breed son of an Army washer woman squaw.

Run!

Chapter 14

Longarm stood at the top of a rocky buttress and gazed intently back to the south as the sun lifted on the eastern horizon. Molly studied his face and then said, "How many riders do you count?"

"Five."

"Me, too. I guess that leaves no doubt who is coming to lift our scalps."

"You're right. Those Navajo are really going to be loaded for bear this time," Longarm told her. "We beat them at their own game. They've been insulted and will demand more than we can give to keep peace."

"We have two Spencer rifles. If necessary, can't we ambush them?"

"If we did that, we'd be crossing the line among their people. We'd be bringing the entire Navajo nation down on us."

"Well, we can't just let them rob and punish us! And we can't outrun them riding double. So what do you propose?"

"I don't propose anything except to keep moving. I do know that laying our weapons down and giving them these horses and all our weapons—even if that would be enough satisfaction—would be a fatal mistake."

"I'm glad to hear *that*," Molly told him. "Because I'm in no mood to put myself at their mercy. I well remember hearing their angry howls when we stampeded their ponies out of that corral and then ran them over. I wouldn't be surprised if at least a few of them are suffering more than just injuries to their pride."

Longarm gazed north. "We can't be far from the Four Corners. Trouble is, I have no idea where the Hooker headquarters is to be found. It might even be way up in Colorado."

"That's not what Mike's letter said."

"True," Longarm agreed, "but these gangs move often. If they are stealing lots of horses and cattle and altering brands and reselling them, they might have a hideout clear up in Utah or someplace we don't even know about yet."

Molly sighed. "Listen, why don't we just forget about all those possible complications and get moving. We can cover ten or fifteen miles before those Navajo overtake and try to rob and maybe even kill us. Perhaps something good will happen in the meantime."

"Like what?" Longarm deadpanned.

"I don't know! Are there any army forts closer than Fort Wingate?"

"Not to my knowledge. There might be an Indian agency up there someplace, but it would take pure luck to find it, and even then you never know what to expect."

"You mean an Indian agent might side with those five thieving Navajo?"

"If he wants to keep his scalp, he might."

Molly looked disgusted and shook her head. "No sense standing here and talking, is there?"

"Nope."

Longarm tightened his cinch and mounted his lame horse.

"What are you doing?"

"This fella has a stone bruise, not a broken leg. I'm going to make him carry me a few miles before we start

129

wearing down your mount by riding double."

"But—"

"Yeah," Longarm said, "it's going to hurt the animal worse than if we were leading him, but things are hard on everyone out here. So don't pity the beast, because it's not my fault he went and threw a shoe."

Molly's eyebrows shot up. "Are you suggesting that it's the *horse's* fault?"

"You drive me crazy sometimes," Longarm said, mounting his lame animal and kicking it into a limping trot. "Come on!"

Molly didn't have to be told twice. She checked her own cinch, jammed the toe of her boot into the wooden stirrup of the Indian saddle and hurried to catch up with Longarm. Bouncing along, she gritted her teeth and tried to ease her bottom's hammering against the brittle rawhide saddle. Riding bareback again, she decided, would almost be a blessing.

They kept up a steady, punishing pace into the early afternoon and must have glanced back over their shoulders a thousand times. The five Navajo riders were gaining and were now in plain view.

"What are we going to do!" Molly cried in pain and exasperation. "We can't just let them overtake us and shoot us out of our saddles!"

"I'm thinking!"

"Think faster! Custis, we desperately need a plan!"

Longarm didn't have the heart to tell Molly that there really was no good plan for this predicament. The facts of their situation were simple and awful. They were about to be overtaken. When that happened, the Navajo might kill them and they might not—but Longarm was betting that they'd try.

"You see those high rocks up ahead about a mile?" he shouted.

"Of course!"

"That's where we're going to make our stand."

"But what about water? They could wait us out and we'd die of thirst!"

"Yeah, that'd be how I'd handle it if I were them."

"Custis!"

"It's the best that I can do," he yelled, driving his laboring horse toward the hillock and marshaling the last of its strength and will.

Molly was close on his heels, and the Navajo, now realizing Custis's intentions, tried hard to overtake them on the flats.

"They're going to catch us!"

"No they won't!"

Rifle fire split the great expanse of silence.

"They're going to shoot us!"

"No they aren't!"

"Why not?"

"Because you can't hit anything off the back of a running horse. Come on, Molly, don't fold on me now!"

The bullets were whistling all around them, and one even grazed Longarm's lame mount, creating a sudden burst of speed that nearly flipped him backwards over the miserable Indian saddle. But somehow they reached the high rocks, and Longarm shouted, "Molly, take care of our horses!"

He grabbed both rifles and took a firing position on the rocks. Without hesitating, Longarm put a warning shot in front of the lead Navajo rider. The slug was so close that the rider drew up sharply and the others did the same as more bullets whip-cracked through their midst, kicking up clouds of dust under the bellies of their ponies.

The Indians beat a hasty retreat out of firing range.

Longarm hurried back into the rocks to help Molly. "Let's hobble these horses and keep them back far enough so they can't be shot."

"Do you think the Navajo would do that?"

"I don't know, but why take a chance?"

They got their horses hobbled and securely tethered.

Both animals were drenched with sweat and were very nervous, but there was no way they could escape. Longarm and Molly then returned to a good vantage point up in the rocks and saw that the Navajo were bunched together, trying to figure out their next move.

"What do you think will happen now?" Molly asked.

"If I were them, I'd split up and surround us. Then wait it out until we have to surrender or die of thirst."

"Do you think that's what—"

"Molly, I don't know. But why risk getting shot when a few days in the hot sun without water would do just as well?"

"Look! One is taking the canteens and riding away."

"He's headed for the nearest water hole," Longarm said. "Now what do you want to bet that the other four are going to split up and circle this rocky prominence. They'll just wait us out."

"We're cooked," Molly whispered, her eyes wet with tears. "After all that we've gone through, we're cooked."

"No we're not," Longarm grated. "Two can play this game."

"What do you mean?"

"We'll just settle back and wait until it gets dark," Longarm suggested.

"Do we have any choice?"

"No."

Molly got up and went back to loosen their cinches. She returned with two half-empty canteens. "There isn't enough water here to last us two days. And that's not even considering the horses."

"We've got to go after them tonight," Longarm said. "They'll be expecting it, but we have no choice other than to run or to fight. We lose for certain if we don't take action."

"All right, then, let's do it," Molly said.

Longarm watched her take a couple of sips from the canteen.

132

"Your turn," she said.

"Thanks, but I'm not thirsty yet."

"Sure you are."

"I'm sleepy," he said, glancing up at the sun and judging it to be about four o'clock. "Spell me for a couple hours, and then I'll do the same for you."

"All right. But don't you think they might start sneaking up on us?"

"No, but keep a sharp lookout."

Molly raised her head up and exclaimed, "Uh-oh. They're splitting up just like you figured!"

"Stop worrying so much."

"But shouldn't we do *something*!"

He yawned, stretched out in the shade of the rocks and thought about that for a moment before saying, "I'll put some thought to that directly."

"Dammit, Custis, you'll be *asleep* directly."

"I suppose. Don't let them get in amongst us, Molly. You've got that good shooting eye. If they come in close, shoot to kill."

"Count on it."

The sun was going down when she woke Longarm. "I can't see any of them now. They've all disappeared."

Longarm checked his weapons and studied the sky. "It will be dark soon, and then we'll make our move."

"All right," she replied, not sounding very hopeful.

Longarm didn't like waiting around and wondering if the Navajo were sneaking in for a killing shot. He grew impatient, and when he supposed it was around ten o'clock, whispered, "All right, Molly. Let's move!"

They started to creep out of the rocks when, suddenly, Molly cried, "Custis, look out!"

Longarm hadn't seen the Indian lying on top of a huge boulder with a rifle pointed down at them. One second he was being yelled at; the next, shot at. The bullet grazed his shoulder, and he lost his balance and fell hard. Molly's rifle boomed, and the Indian screamed and then tumbled off the boulder to land with a thud and a gasp only a few yards away.

"Are you all right?" Molly asked, tearing a pistol from the Indian's belt.

"I'm not sure," Longarm replied, inspecting his wound and then wiping his blood on his pants. "I think you just saved my bacon."

"Well, you've saved mine, so now we're even. And guess what?"

"What?"

"He was carrying a Colt revolver. It's not mine, but it sure will do!"

Longarm knelt beside the dead Navajo. "We're in for it now," he said. "Not that we weren't before. But after this, there will be no quarter asked and none given. Stealing back our horses was one thing, killing one of them quite another."

"We had no choice." Molly pulled a handkerchief out of her pants and pressed it down on the bullet wound. "We have even less now."

Longarm started to say more, but his words were disrupted when more bullets poured down from the rocks. Grabbing Molly's hand, he propelled her under a rock and jumped in behind.

"We should have moved quicker."

One of their horses whinnied, and they heard the sound of hoofbeats. Longarm cursed silently and said, "They got our horses again! We brought our canteens, didn't we?"

"Custis, I thought you—"

He didn't wait to hear more but instead jumped up and hurried back to their earlier vantage point. The canteens and even their food were missing.

Molly was right behind him. "I guess we're not doing this very well, huh?"

Longarm eased under a boulder and pulled the woman close. "Don't start blaming yourself, because this is my fault. I should have checked to make sure one of us had the canteens. But now, we've got no choice except to get out of this death trap before it's too late. We're both expert rifle shots, and I think we have the advantage out in the open.''

"If the one that went for water isn't back, there are only three left," Molly reasoned aloud. "I like those odds."

"So do I. Let's see if we can get off this hillock and out on the flats. We might as well head off in the same direction as the one who went for water."

"I agree."

"Let's go, then," he told her. "When the sun comes up tomorrow, we'll either be dead or mighty thirsty."

"Maybe neither." Molly squeezed his hand. "If the water hole is nearby."

"I hope so," Longarm said. "We sure could use a few good breaks. Stay low and right behind me. Now!"

They kept to the shadows, certain that, at any moment, the night silence would be shattered by gunfire. But that never happened, and they managed to get off the rocky prominence and down on the sagebrush flats.

"That way," Longarm said, taking a bearing on the North Star and squinting hard to see the tracks of the Navajo who had been sent for water.

It took him an hour to find those tracks, and then they hurried along.

"How is your shoulder wound?" Molly asked around midnight.

"It's doing just fine, thank you."

"Do you think they're following us?"

Longarm jumped up on a rock and peered along the path they'd come. "Don't see 'em."

"Why would they just let us go?"

"I can't answer that. Maybe they're saying prayers over the one that you shot. Maybe they just don't want to risk being shot themselves. But you can bet they'll be back on our trail come sunup."

"Should we be trying to hide our footprints?"

"Wouldn't work. They'd find them, and besides, pretty quick they'll figure out we are following that other fella, hoping to find the nearest source of water."

"When we do," Molly said, "that's where we can make a real stand. With water we can hold out for days."

"But no food. We forgot that, too."

"Then shoot something," Molly told him. "Or I will."

"Such as?"

"I don't know. A tortoise or a coyote or maybe a prairie chicken we could roast."

"I'm afraid there are no prairie chickens in this country. No sage hens or any other fowl that is good to eat."

"What about a snake?"

"I've heard they can be eaten."

"Then we'll look for a snake or a turtle or something like that," Molly said. "And we'll just hang on and pray that help arrives."

Longarm didn't say anything about that because, as far as he was concerned, there wasn't a Chinaman's chance that they'd get any help in this killing country.

Chapter 15

"Molly, did you see that!"

She had been plodding wearily along with her eyes fixed to the ground. The urgency in Longarm's voice caused her head to snap up. "See what?"

"Movement up ahead."

"Maybe it was a burro or—"

Longarm grabbed Molly's arm and dragged her into the brush and then pushed her down to a crouch. He whispered in her ear. "A rider is coming, so watch carefully. He's just disappeared in a low stretch of ground, but when he comes out again, you'll see him highlighted by the moon."

"Who . . . the fifth Navajo?"

"Who else? And, Molly, he'd be the answer to our prayers."

They remained crouched in the brush until the rider reappeared, seeming to lift out of the earth. He was still a half-mile distant, and had there not been a bright moon overhead, Longarm doubted they would have even seen him.

"What are we going to do?" Molly asked.

"We need his horse and the water he's bringing back."

"We're going to have to kill him."

"I don't think so," Longarm told her, "but you can be sure he'll kill us in a heartbeat if he gets the chance."

"Then, what?"

"You could wing him just bad enough to knock him off his pony."

"Me?!"

Even in semi-darkness, Longarm noted how Molly's eyes widened with shock. "You're the crack shot. You proved it."

"But what if I miss . . . or accidentally kill him?"

"If you miss and he escapes, we're sunk. If you kill him, well, girl, we all make mistakes."

"Custis!"

He grabbed her firmly by the shoulders. "Listen, Molly. We are running out of time. This Navajo's friends tried to kill us, and he will too, given half a chance. We can't afford to fail. This is the break that we've both been praying for, and we might not get another."

"All right. I'll do it," she agreed. "Where should I aim?"

Longarm thought for a moment. If the Navajo water bearer had been on foot, the preferred spot to wound him would be the leg. But since the Navajo was mounted, the target was different. "Shoot him in the shoulder. As far out as you can, but don't miss."

"If I do?"

"Then we have to shoot to kill. That's not what we want, but there is no room for any more mistakes."

"You mean like the one you made in leaving our canteens behind?"

Longarm scowled. "That's right."

"I'm sorry," Molly apologized, hugging his neck. "Custis, that was mean, and I take my words back."

"No hard feelings," he told her. "Leaving the canteens was my fault. I haven't done much of anything right since we've been on this trail together. But I do know we've got to stop this man right now and grab both his water and his

138

pony if we want any chance of escaping the ones on our trail.''

"I won't miss," Molly promised. "And once he's down, you run up and knock him out and then catch his pony."

"I will, even if I have to chase it five miles," Longarm vowed. "Would you feel more comfortable doing this with the Spencer?"

"No. There's more of a chance that it is inaccurate or might even misfire. This Colt revolver won't fail."

"All right then, as soon as you fire, I'll take care of the rest."

So they crouched near the trail they'd been following and waited in the semi-darkness. Longarm could almost feel Molly's tension; she began to take deep, calming breaths as she cocked back the hammer of her six-gun.

"You okay?"

"Yeah, but I almost wish I had to shoot fast. I've never had so much time to aim as I'll have now."

"If you miss, I'll back you up," Longarm reassured her. "Surely both of us won't miss."

"Shhh! Maybe he heard us!"

Longarm was afraid the Navajo might have heard their whispers because he suddenly drew rein and dismounted. Longarm and Molly ducked low and held their breath, but a moment later they heard the Indian passing water. This was followed by a grunt of satisfaction and then another of effort as the Navajo remounted and continued toward them.

"Now," Longarm breathed, "just take your time and aim for the shoulder. It ought to be real easy."

Molly raised up, slowly took aim and squeezed off a round. "Oh my gawd!" she cried, "Custis, I missed!"

Longarm saw the Indian try to dismount and fired. The Navajo howled, grabbed his shoulder and pitched to the ground. Longarm vaulted over the rock they'd been hiding behind and landed upon the wounded Indian as he struggled to tear his gun free. He pistol-whipped the Navajo into unconsciousness.

"Is he dead?" Molly cried, running over to join them.

"I don't have time to find out. I have to catch his pony!"

At the sound of gunfire, the Navajo's horse had whirled and galloped off a short ways. Now it stood frightened with nostrils twitching at the scent of fresh blood. Longarm could see a cluster of canteens tied to the Indian saddle and guessed there were at least ten as he slowly advanced on the spooked animal.

"Easy, boy," he said in a low, soothing voice. "I won't hurt you."

The pony was scrawny and jug-headed with a bowed neck and crooked legs. As Longarm crept forward, it began to back away, its eyes rolling with fear and distrust.

"Take it easy, boy," he urged trying to keep his voice calm and steady. "Everything is all right."

But the pony whirled and trotted off, waving its big head as if in contradiction.

"Stop!" Longarm shouted, sprinting forward in an attempt to grab the animal.

It was a mistake. The horse ran a good quarter mile before it stopped and twisted around to see if it was still being chased. Longarm bit back his anger and hurried forward, but when he grew near, the animal trotted off again. It soon became apparent that the more Longarm chased the pony, the more it would run.

"Damn you!" he cussed, bending over with his hands on his bent knees and gasping for breath.

"Custis!"

He twisted around to look back the way he'd come.

"Custis, this poor man is really bleeding!"

Longarm glared at the spooked pony, and it seemed to glare back as if wondering whether this game was finished.

"Custis! I need your help!"

He shuffled back to Molly, his breath like fire in his lungs. When he knelt down beside the fallen Indian, he saw that the man was bleeding.

"What are we going to do! We can't just let him die."

"Let's bandage him up," Longarm decided. "That's all we have time for."

"But he'll die if your bullet isn't removed!"

"Not true. I've known a lot of men who have lived long lives carrying lead from bullet wounds."

"You have?"

"Yes."

Longarm tore away the Indian's shirt and ripped it into bandaging. He used the man's belt to fasten the crude bandaging in place. It would have helped to keep pressure applied to control the bleeding, but that simply was not an option.

"He's probably going to bleed to death," Molly fretted out loud.

"Look," Longarm said, trying not to lose his patience, "this Indian would have killed us without a moment's hesitation."

"That doesn't matter, Custis. We ambushed him! He never had a chance."

"And neither will we if we don't stop jawin'! Molly, I guarantee his friends are coming, and they might have heard our shots. So let's get moving before it's too late."

Longarm placed a rock to weigh down the bandage in the futile hope that it would stanch the bleeding. Then he pulled Molly erect and gave her a rough shove in the direction of the Indian's pony. "Let's concentrate on catching that horse."

"Maybe this man's friends will appear soon and save him," Molly sniffled. "He was awful young, Custis. Maybe not even as old as I am."

Longarm almost had to drag her away from the wounded man. He also felt bad about the Navajo and wanted to say something that would raise Molly's spirits. "Listen, I really expect he'll pull through."

"Custis, you aren't just saying that to make me feel better, are you?"

"Hell, no! Indians are tough, and his friends know how

141

to make strong medicines from plants and stuff they can gather all around themselves. They even might take him to some old Navajo medicine man and give up chasing us.''

''I hadn't thought of that!'' Molly brightened. ''Oh, I sure hope so. And I'm sorry that I missed. We're just both real run down and tired, Custis. That's why we keep making mistakes. We need to rest.''

''No time for that.''

''I know, but that don't change the needing.''

''I sure wish I could have grabbed that pony and the canteens.''

''We'll catch him, I think. I'm pretty good with horses.''

''Glad to hear that, because this one sure doesn't like my looks.''

''Wish I had a carrot or an apple, though. Even some sugar would help. Look, there he is waiting for us just up the trail.''

''Sure,'' Longarm said cryptically, ''he thinks this is some kind of game. Wait until you get close—he'll whirl and run. Then stop and wait, then run again. If we didn't need that jug-head, I'd put a bullet through his fevered brain.''

''No! He's scared.''

''He's laughing at us,'' Longarm growled.

''I've got an idea. Maybe if we both rushed it at the very same time . . .''

''Forget that,'' Longarm told her. ''The only thing we can hope for is that he leads us to the nearest water.''

''I hope that isn't *too* far.''

''Me, too,'' Longarm replied. ''Because those Navajo can't be very far behind.''

The Indian pony did lead them straight to water. Then, satisfied with its surroundings and perhaps wearying of its game, the pony dropped its ugly head and began to graze.

Longarm ignored the beast as he and Molly drank their fill of water and surveyed their surroundings. This spring bubbled out of the rocks and went underground to feed a bowl-shaped meadow no larger than a small pasture where the pony was grazing. Pines surrounded the grass, and the charred remainders of many campfires gave evidence that this was a popular camp.

Longarm bathed his face and then watched sunrise struggle to gild the eastern horizon. It would be daylight in fifteen or twenty minutes, and there was no telling how far behind the Navajo were and when they would attack. His suggestion to Molly that The Navajo might abandon the chase and seek a medicine man raised her spirits, but was improbable. Longarm was quite sure that the Indians would arrive to avenge the one that Molly had shot in the high rocks, as well as their wounded companion.

When the sunlight grew bolder, Longarm hiked up to the spring, which offered little more than a rivulet this late in the summer. The life-giving water bubbled out from under a fallen pine, and the area was littered with deadfall and rocks. This pleased Longarm because the spring was where they had to make their stand, and whoever controlled the water controlled time. Sure, it would have been better to take the highest nearby ground, but there was enough cover to protect them from any angle. If the Navajo failed to recapture either their canteens or access to the spring, they would either have to leave or die of thirst.

In the desert, whoever had water had life.

Longarm pressed his shoulder against a boulder and felt it rock ever so slightly. He repeated this test with several other large rocks that hung precariously on the steep hillside near the spring. If their situation became desperate, they might be able to blunt an attack from the meadow below by rolling these rocks down on the Navajo and their onrushing ponies. But more likely, the Indians would surround him and Molly and try to finish them off under a murderous crossfire.

Think about this, though, he told himself. *First there were five. Then there were four, and now there are only three. You and Molly can handle the Navajo. You've got the water, you've got rifles and pistols and you can win this fight if they don't bring a bunch of their friends and surround you like General Custer at the Little Big Horn.*

Longarm hurried down to the pasture and was heartened to see that Molly had finally lured the ugly pony into her clutches. She had roped him to a pine tree and was already removing the canteens.

"We'll tote them up to the spring."

"Why would we need them?"

"We won't," he told her, "but *they* will."

Molly nodded with understanding. "I even found two dead rabbits in a pack tied to the saddle. They look awfully skinny, but I'm famished. Custis, do you think we'd have time to roast them and eat 'em before the trouble starts?"

"I'm sure of it," he said, taking the canteens and the canvas bag with the dead rabbits and starting back up toward the spring. "So what if they see our smoke? It's not like we could go into hiding up here."

"What about the pony? If we leave it tied here, they'll steal it back again."

"Let them." Longarm slung the canteens around his neck and headed back up the steep hillside to the spring. "If they want that jug-head, it'll be their misfortune and none of our own."

"He led us to this spring, didn't he?"

"Sure," Longarm called back over his shoulder. "And the next thing I hear is how you'll be telling me he did it to help us. Right?"

Molly shouted back. "I know that you're not a in a very good mood, but you don't have to be so sarcastic!"

"Sorry," he called, "but let's get a fire going and eat before we have those unwelcome guests arriving at our little hillside party."

Molly said something else, but Longarm suspected it was not worth hearing.

144

Chapter 16

They feasted on the skinny rabbits and talked about their childhoods and about how things hadn't worked out as planned.

"Custis, I doubt I'll ever marry that rancher and have a bunch of kids," Molly said. "But I've been thinking of moving to Denver."

"Oh?"

"That's right. I've heard that it's a nice town with lots of eligible bachelors."

"I wouldn't know about that."

"Do you think I could get a job in Denver?"

"I expect so. Doing what?"

"Maybe opening my own business." Molly frowned thoughtfully. "A cafe would be nice. Or a dress shop, perhaps."

"Well, there's shops of every kind already in Denver, but I guess there's always room for one more."

"What about *us*?"

He shrugged. "I'd like to see you come to Denver. But most of the time I'm traveling."

"Yes, and I'll bet you already have a bunch of pretty lady friends and admirers in Denver, huh?"

Longarm was getting a bit uncomfortable. "Molly," he

said, "this is a free country, and Colorado is a fine place to live. Denver is a big town, and a gal like you could find a lot more opportunities there than in Flagstaff. But I don't want you coming to Denver because of me."

"Oh, no! That's not it at all. I just thought you might know a few people that could help me find work. And, of course, maybe we could go out once in a while, but only with the understanding that we'd each have our own lives."

"Sure." Longarm smiled with relief. "I might even be able to help you get on with the federal government. Can you type?"

"No."

"Well, if you can spell pretty good, there's always office work."

"I spell fine."

"Then I'll see what I can do when we get there."

"And we can go out once in a while together on the town?"

"You bet!"

Molly took his hand. "You're a good man, Custis. But you sure don't like being crowded by a woman."

"No," he told her, "I don't. But you're not crowding me now, are you?"

"Uh-uh." Molly placed his hand on her bosom. "Maybe we have some free time to ourselves this afternoon. I mean, we can't sleep, and we might as well have a nice time together."

He scooted over close and unbuttoned her shirt. "I think you've got something here, Molly."

They kissed, their lips coated with slippery rabbit grease. Then Longarm unbuttoned her blouse and quickly got Molly aroused by licking her nipples until they stood up like cherries.

"Oh, my," she breathed, slipping her hand down his pants and discovering his erection. "What do we have here?"

"Open the package and find out."

146

Molly unbuttoned his pants, and then he unbuttoned her pants, and pretty soon they were making love again by the spring, up on the hillside among the rocks. Longarm took his time with Molly, unwilling to rush what could be their last tryst. But pretty soon they were thrusting and gasping, and when he felt her body quiver with release and heard her cry out in ecstasy, he unleashed a torrent and filled her with his hot seed.

For a long while they lay content in each other's arms, but then Longarm had an uneasy feeling that they were not alone. It wasn't just a vague, undefined feeling, either. It was an immediate, urgent premonition that he had better get his pants on and grab his gun.

"What's wrong?" Molly asked.

"I think we have company." He pulled up his pants and buckled his belt. Shirtless, he lifted up a ways, whispering, "Molly, stay down."

"Do you see anyone?"

"No, but I'm almost certain I heard something up above in the trees. I think they're moving into positions all around us."

"What—"

"It can't be helped," he told her, his gun now held tightly in his fist. "There is no way that we could have prevented them from surrounding us."

"Do you see one?"

"Not yet. Let me have one of those Spencers."

Molly checked the rifle to make sure that it was ready to fire. She took the other rifle, but not before she buttoned her shirt and pulled up her pants. "No matter what else happens here, my darling, that was terrific lovemaking."

"Yeah, it was, wasn't it. Maybe we can do it again tonight."

"If we live that long. Do you think they'll attack?"

"Not if we can either kill or run them off."

"I wouldn't think we'd have a very good chance of doing that."

But Longarm thought different. He detected movement out of the corner of his eye and snapped off a shot just as a Navajo opened fire. Longarm felt a shard of rock lance his cheek, but the Indian went down thrashing. He could have finished the man off but held his fire.

"One of his friends will be along to fetch him," Longarm said tightly, as he brought his finger away from his cheek covered with blood. "And when he does, put a bullet in him."

"Dammit, let me see that cheek."

"It's just a scratch."

"I'll be the judge of that." Molly tore a piece of her sleeve away and used a rag to dampen it from one of the canteens. "You're just lucky that it didn't get you in the eye," she said after wiping away the blood.

"Get ready to fire," he ordered. "You won't have but a split second."

"I don't want to kill these people. It's Yancy Hooker that—"

"Molly, this is war, and in war, you often don't get second chances. So shoot the next one that comes into view, knowing that's one less who can kill us."

"All right."

A quarter hour passed, and the silence deepened as Longarm and Molly crouched in readiness. His facial wound finally stopped bleeding, but it left a painful throbbing in his cheek. The Indian he'd shot had stopped moving, and Longarm was thinking he was most likely dead when he saw motion in the brush near the fallen man.

"Here we go," he grated. "Take aim and make it count."

The Indian that dashed out to grab his wounded friend was smallish and wore a red shirt and bandanna around his neck. Longarm remembered him as little more than a kid. Maybe that's why neither of them could cut him down. Instead they watched him grab his friend and drag him into cover. A moment later, they heard a mournful howl and then a chant.

"Custis, what is going on?"

"I must have killed the first one," Longarm replied. "I've heard enough Indians to recognize a death song."

"That means there are only two left, doesn't it?"

"Yes, unless they got reinforcements."

"I doubt that they've had time."

"These people *make* time. They're patient and won't give up."

Tears rolled down Molly's cheeks. "This isn't anything like I'd planned."

"I know. When the lead starts flying, your best plans go right out the window. At least they always have for me."

"So what do we do now?"

"We wait and let them make the next move." Longarm took a deep breath. "They've got our money, our saddles, bedrolls, food, cooking utensils and horses. If they're smart, they'll cut their losses and leave."

"Would you do that after two of your friends were shot and another wounded?"

"Nope, but Indians are smarter than I am when it comes to many things. If you read the dime novels, you'd think that they don't care about living or dying, but that isn't even the slightest bit true. I've seen plenty of Indians, and they don't want to die anymore than we do."

"Are they braver than most whites?"

"I can't answer that," Longarm replied. "But they are more spiritual."

"What do you mean?"

"Most Indians believe that about everything above, below and on the earth has its own spirit."

"You mean animals like deer and bear?"

"And trees, rocks, water, sky and even the sun and the moon. There's nothing that they don't believe has a spirit. Christians, on the other hand, pretty much believe in God and his son, Jesus."

"What do you believe in?"

"When I get in a tight spot, I mostly just believe in myself."

"I believe in God, and I'm going to start praying more if we survive."

"That can't hurt, Molly. I've been known to say a few last prayers myself."

They waited and waited but saw nothing more as the death chant continued until dark. Then the night suddenly went silent.

"Custis, will they try to sneak in and kill us in the dark?"

"We have to assume they might."

"Then we need to stand watches and take turns sleeping."

"Fine. Go to sleep."

"No, you first," Molly argued. "I'm not sleepy yet. And that death chant has really unnerved me."

"Okay," he agreed, "but if you accidentally fall asleep, it could cost us our lives."

"I know. And I'd give anything for a pot of coffee. But I'm really wide awake."

Longarm yawned. He glanced up at the North Star and wondered exactly where the deuce they were in respect to the Four Corners.

"All right," he said. "Wake me when your chin starts bouncing off that pretty chest."

"You think it's nice, huh?"

"Real nice."

"Maybe you'd even like to kiss my chest goodnight."

"Molly, I . . ."

She unbuttoned her shirt and exposed her breasts. Longarm dutifully kissed both her nipples and then said, "I got to sleep now."

"I know. I just wanted you to do that because I knew it would get me excited so I'd be able to stay awake longer."

"Oh."

Longarm lay down between the rocks with one of the cool, wet canteens as his pillow and immediately fell asleep.

Molly awakened him saying, "Custis, I can't stay awake any longer."

He roused from a deep slumber and sat up, rubbing his eyes. "Any sign of 'em?"

"No. I haven't heard a sound. Maybe you were right and they've gone to find a medicine man."

"I hope so, but don't count on it," he told her. "Now, lie down and get some shut-eye. I'll wake you at dawn just in case that's when they decide to attack."

"All right."

Longarm took a sip from his canteen and then extracted a half-smoked cigar from his shirt pocket and smoked a while, listening for movement in the brush. He didn't hear a sound and spent some time analyzing their predicament from every angle. The way he saw things right now, there could not be more than two Navajo from the original bunch of five, and they'd have to know there would be a very stiff price to pay if they tried to rush the spring.

If I were them, I'd cut my losses and give it up, he thought. *But then, if I were them, I wouldn't be in this fix.*

Sunrise bathed the hard, dry land in soft, glowing colors, and when Longarm raised his head to look for the Navajo, he didn't see any. That did not mean that they weren't waiting to ambush him if he left his nearly impregnable position, but he was beginning to think that they were alone when he saw a faint rooster tail of dust on the southern horizon.

He resisted waking Molly because there was no point in depriving her of another half hour of much-needed sleep. And, after a while, it was obvious that what he had initially thought were more Navajo was just a lone rider coming fast with several mounts in tow.

Longarm frowned and drank from his canteen as the rider

grew closer until there was something familiar about the way he . . .

"Redbow!" Longarm grinned so hard that his lips split, but he didn't care. "Molly, wake up. The cavalry has finally arrived!"

At just that instant, a puff of rifle smoke erupted from the trees. Longarm saw Redbow rein his mount sharply and then disappear around a ridge.

"What's going on?" Molly asked, still mostly asleep.

"Redbow was coming to the rescue, but then one of the Navajo took a shot at him out in the valley."

"And?"

"He missed, and Redbow disappeared up there by where that huge boulder stands in front of those trees."

"We had better help him."

Molly started to rise, but Longarm grabbed and pulled her back down. "Easy," he said. "I have a feeling our friend can take care of himself."

"But there's *two* of them out there someplace."

They both heard a series of shots, followed by silence.

"What?"

"I have no idea," Longarm said. "But, if I were to guess, I'd bet on Redbow rather than the Navajo."

"How can we just sit and wait?"

"How?" Longarm shrugged his broad shoulders. "Why would we want to go charging out of here and risk getting shot? Redbow is either dead or alive. If he's dead, we can't help him, and if he's alive, he'll find us before long."

"You sure have a way of simplifying complex and important things," Molly groused. "He's our friend and—"

"Don't fool yourself, Molly. Unless I'm badly mistaken, Redbow isn't anyone's friend. Oh, maybe he is to the Hopi, but he sure isn't our friend. If he helps us, it's because that is in his best interests. Not because he either likes or feels any sense of loyalty."

"I strongly disagree!"

"That's okay by me, but I am just saying that you had

152

better not count on him to save your hide. He'll do it only if it serves his purpose, which is to kill Yancy Hooker and probably all of his brothers and blood relatives."

Molly clamped her jaw shut and said no more. They waited about twenty minutes and then Redbow came riding around the point and into view.

"He either killed 'em or ran 'em off," Longarm said, coming to his feet and emerging from their little rock fortress. "It's safe to go down now."

When they got down to the grassy place, Redbow was hobbling the three horses he'd delivered.

"Jumped the gun a little, didn't you?" Longarm asked.

"Five days was too long."

"Maybe a mite."

Redbow sat down in the grass cross-legged, and Longarm sat down in front of him asking, "Did you kill the last two Navajo?"

"Yes."

"That's what I thought."

"We go after Yancy Hooker and men now."

"Yeah," Longarm agreed, picking up the Spencer rifles, "it's way past time for a Four Corners showdown."

Chapter 17

They passed over Black Mesa and then moved down into Four Corners, splashing across the shallow San Juan River and galloping into the dry and forbidding southwest corner of Colorado. This was a wild, sparsely inhabited land characterized by canyons and deep arroyos that flooded in springtime and went dry by early summer. Longarm didn't much care for it and wondered how a cattleman could survive when the country appeared that it would have trouble supporting even sheep or goats.

None of that mattered now, because they had spotted a ranch hidden up a long, narrow canyon. And it wasn't just some little family operation, either. Longarm could see that a stream flowed for better than a mile down the center of the canyon, creating a wide band of grass upon which maybe fifty horses and twice that many cattle now grazed in the morning sun. A ranch house was placed at the far end of the canyon, and around it were corrals and three or four outbuildings that Longarm imagined were the usual bunkhouse, blacksmith, saddle and feed storage areas.

"It looks pretty prosperous for this hard country," Molly said, breaking the silence. "Custis, what do you think?"

"It might belong to the Hookers," Longarm said. "I guess we are going to have to investigate and find out."

"I will go up there," Redbow told them, as he pointed to the mesa tops that ringed the canyon. "I will see if it is the Four Corners Gang led by Hooker men."

"Oh, no," Longarm told him. "If anyone goes up there to spy on the place, *I'll* do it."

Redbow shook his head vigorously. "You stay, I go."

"Sorry," Longarm grated. "But I'm calling the shots. Remember?"

For a moment Longarm thought he was in for a fight, but then Molly cried, "Oh for heaven's sakes, this is no time to quarrel! Why don't you *both* go up there and figure it out. I'll wait down here with the horses."

"I'm not too sure that would be safe," Longarm told her as he unclenched his fists.

But Molly was insistent. "I'll be well armed and hidden, so that if anyone comes or goes, they'll never see me back in these pinions."

Longarm reconsidered. "All right. But if something goes wrong, you stay hidden until we return."

"The only thing that could go wrong is if they see you climbing around up there on the mesa. I'll be fine."

Longarm glanced at Redbow, who was already leading his horse deeper into the trees.

"I don't much care for him," Longarm said more to himself than to Molly.

"It doesn't matter, does it? We need him, and he needs us."

"Maybe, but maybe not."

"Listen, Custis, Redbow knows that he can't do this by himself, and he also knows that having the law on his side could eventually make a big difference."

"I hope that's the way he's thinking."

"I'm sure it is."

"Here," Longarm said, handing his reins to Molly and dragging his rifle from its boot. "I have a feeling that our half-breed friend is going to put me to shame when the climbing begins."

155

"Go at your pace, not his."

"I will," Longarm vowed. "I don't know how he recovered from that bullet wound in the leg so fast."

"Maybe he knows some Indian medicines."

"Yeah, that would explain it."

Longarm didn't like the idea of leaving Molly on her own, but the thought of allowing Redbow to go up on the mesa by himself was even less appealing. The man had blood in his eye and murder in his heart. Longarm would not put it past him to execute Yancy Hooker should he have half a chance.

"We'll be back down sometime tonight. Tomorrow morning at the latest."

"Good luck to you both."

"We'll just make sure these are the ones we want," Longarm told her. "If it's an honest ranching operation, they'll never even know we were up there watching."

"I understand. Just . . . just be careful."

"You, too," he said. "You've got plenty of water and cover. Stay low and wait for our return."

"I will," she promised. "But just remember, I've got a rifle and a pistol, and I'm not one bit defenseless."

"I know that."

Longarm couldn't think of anything else to say, so he headed after Redbow before the man got an insurmountable head start.

After they left, Molly set to arranging their camp. There really wasn't much to arrange, but she was nervous and needed to keep busy. After things were in order, she still felt restless, so she went back down to the edge of the trees. This was tough country, and she wondered if there were any white women within fifty miles and decided that they probably were not.

Molly found a nice, comfortable place in the rocks where she could rest in the warm afternoon sun. A soft breeze riffled through the pines, and when she gazed into the peaceful valley, Molly found it difficult to believe that this might be a hideout for the Four Corners Gang.

I'll bet anything it belongs to some honest, hard-working ranching family, she thought.

Molly must have dozed off for a while because when she awakened, four cowboys were driving a large band of horses straight for the mouth of the canyon.

She sat up quickly, thinking, *they could be mustangers. Maybe that's how they make most of their earnings. On the other hand, they might be horse thieves.*

Molly ducked her head when the two cowboys reined up at the mouth of the canyon and started talking. They were still about a quarter mile away, so she felt confident of her hiding place. Molly squinted hard, but they were too far away for her to recognize. She peeked over the rocks and up toward the ranch buildings. Several men had emerged and were heading for the corral, probably to help with this band of new horses.

I wonder what is going on.

She was content to stay hidden and allow events to unfold, but suddenly one of their own animals caught the scent of the other horses and began to whinny.

Oh my gawd, we're downwind of that bunch!

Molly almost made the mistake of jumping up to quiet her horses. Instead, she crawled out of the rocks and then scrambled back into the trees. Redbow's little pony was the guilty animal. Even now as Molly raced to clamp a hand over its muzzle, the dun was trumpeting another loud greeting to the horses below.

Molly reached the dun and placed her finger over its soft muzzle. "Easy," she whispered, praying that the riders below had not heard the dun or, if they had, thought it just some wild horse up on the hillside unworthy of their attention.

She closed her eyes and leaned against the dun's shoulder . . . praying with all her might.

157

"Well, would you boys look at that!" a man finally shouted. "What have we found here!"

It *was* the Four Corners Gang, or at least part of it!

Molly lunged for the Spencer she'd left leaning up against a nearby pine. She slammed it to her shoulder, aimed and fired. The lead rider was now whipping his horse and coming fast. Molly's first slug knocked him right over the back of his saddle.

Then everything went crazy. Molly got off a second wild shot that missed before the damned Spencer jammed. She reached for her pistol, but the cowboys were on her so fast that she barely cleared leather. When she brought the six-gun up to fire, Redbow's dun whirled in terror and knocked her spinning to the ground. It was all that she could do to keep from being trampled, much less captured.

"It's her!" a familiar face shouted. "It's the one we had before!"

"Jeb is dead!" someone else bellowed. "She drilled him through the heart!"

One of them yanked Molly up off the ground. She clawed at the big man's eyes, and he bellowed with pain. Then, he grabbed her hair and drew back his fist, and Molly's world exploded in a searing burst of sparks. That was all that she remembered.

They are drowning me, she thought, hearing herself choking into consciousness. *I can't breathe.*

"Wake up!" Bert Hooker shouted.

"Throw another bucket of water in her face!"

Cold water struck Molly like a fist, and she tried to roll and cover her face.

"She's awake now, Bert. Remember her?"

"Damn right! How could any of us forget?"

"But she killed Jeb!"

"I know that, and we're gonna kill her slow. But not before we find out who rode those other two horses. Now, haul her to her feet."

158

Powerful hands dragged Molly erect, and she heard Bert's pistol as he cocked the hammer back. "I might just blow your brains out right now."

"Go ahead!" she coughed.

"You better start talking," Bert warned. "I want to know who else came with you."

"No one!"

He slapped her so hard that her knees buckled, and she tasted fresh blood in her mouth.

"Answer me!"

"Go to hell!" Molly choked. "Shoot me, and let's get this over with!" Molly wasn't afraid of dying, at least not half as much as she was of being used by this bunch of animals again. "Shoot, damn you!"

"Do it, Bert! Splatter her brains all over the gawdamn rocks."

"No," Bert said, dragging her down the hillside to their horses, "we'll kill her slow. When she starts screaming, I reckon it might bring in her friends."

"What about their horses?"

"Put 'em in the corral!"

They tied Molly's hands behind her back and put a noose around her neck. Then Bert mounted his horse, and they dragged her up to the ranch just like they would have treated a steer they meant to slaughter, gut and roast.

"What now?" one of the men asked, grinning wolfishly. "Can we have a taste of her, huh, Bert?"

"No, strip her bare and tie her to a corral post." Bert tilted back his head and gazed up at the mesa top. "They're up there someplace, and I want them to hear her yell and watch her suffer."

"Should we go up after 'em?"

Bert chewed the tip of his mustache. "Let's give them a chance to come to the rescue. If they don't come down by tomorrow morning, we can go up there after 'em. Without horses, they'll be easy to hunt down and kill."

The younger man, whom Molly recognized as one of the

Hookers, chuckled. "I think we are going to have a high old time tonight with this woman."

"I expect so," Bert said. "Yancy and the others will be here tomorrow, and they'll want to use her, so we'd better get all we want tonight."

"Kill me!" Molly shouted. "Kill me!"

"We will," Bert promised, "but we'll do it when there ain't enough of you left even to screw."

Molly fought with every last ounce of her strength, but they made sport of her, tearing away her clothes and pulling off her pants. They dragged her out to the corral and tied her to a post, making crude comments about what they would do to her that night.

Custis, she thought, *if you can see me, put a bullet through my brain and then kill them to the last man. Please, Custis! I'll go mad if they all rape me again!*

Longarm's lungs were on fire as he and Redbow hurried along the rim to arrive at a good vantage point behind the ranch buildings. "Dammit, slow down!"

The half-breed slowed down to a walk and glanced back, saying, "You're soft, Marshal. Way too soft."

Longarm started to reply, and that was when he heard the unmistakable retort of Molly's Spencer rifle. He counted two closely spaced shots. "Dammit, Molly is in trouble!"

Both he and Redbow sprinted over to the rim and saw the riders dragging Molly out of her hiding place. "Damn!" Curtis swore, jumping to his feet.

Redbow tackled him, and Longarm hammered his fist into the side of the half-breed's jaw and then grabbed him by the throat. "Listen, dammit! I know that you don't care about anything except revenge, but they'll torture Molly and drive her insane this time. Don't you understand?"

Redbow struggled to tear Longarm's fingers from his throat but failed. He started to reach for his knife, but Longarm drew his gun and shoved the barrel into his face, hissing, "Don't move, or I swear I'll kill you right now."

Redbow's own powerful body went limp, so Longarm eased his hold, allowing the man to say, "If you kill me, the woman is dead for sure. I'm the only man alive who can go down there and bring her out."

"Maybe. But why would you?"

"To prove that I'm not what you think."

"You're an assassin. You are the judge and the jury and you want Hooker blood."

"Yes! But first, I will save that woman."

Longarm holstered his gun and climbed off the man's chest. They glared at each other for a moment, and then Longarm took a deep breath. "How?"

"Draw some of them up here by firing your rifle. When they come, I'll get the woman free."

"Not a chance."

"Do you have any better idea, Marshal?"

"No."

"Then do as I say."

"I can't trust you."

"You have no other choice. But there is something you must do for me."

"What?"

"If I fail and am captured, you must live long enough to kill me with a bullet to the head."

"All right," Longarm said, as he turned to see Molly being led down the middle of the valley with a noose around her pretty neck, surrounded by the heavily armed outlaws. "I agree to do that. But I'm going to be up here fighting and expect you to do the same down below until the end."

"Until the end," Redbow said quietly, as he gathered his weapons and prepared to make the steep descent into the canyon.

Chapter 18

Longarm lay helplessly watching as Molly was beaten and then stripped and lashed to a corral post. The outlaw leader was a barrel-chested man with long black hair hanging to his shoulder. He swaggered and taunted, poking and pinching Molly and causing her to scream. And sometimes he would turn his attention up to the rim and bellow his mocking laughter until Longarm cursed with frustration.

The distance between himself and the corral was near the limit of Longarm's seven-shot Spencer. An expert marksman might have been able to hit Molly's tormentor, but Longarm figured that his chances were no better than one in three. Those were bad odds, but as the torment continued, Longarm decided that he had nothing to lose and everything to gain by trying what would be a difficult shot. At the worst, he would draw some of the outlaws up to his position, which would be a distraction and help for Redbow. Speaking of long odds, Custis didn't give the halfbreed much chance at all of reaching the canyon floor undetected.

Go ahead and shoot, Longarm told himself as the outlaw leader began slapping Molly again. *At the very worst you'll get his full attention.*

Longarm would have given anything for a powerful .52-

caliber Sharps, whose slug would easily carry across this distance. A Winchester would also have proven superior to the Spencer, but a man had to work with what he had at hand. And so, he levered a shell into the breechloader and began to adjust for a slight breeze and the drop in elevation that always made shooting downward tricky.

About an inch over his head and the same to his left to factor in the wind, Longarm thought as he mentally quieted himself and took careful aim. *And, if you err, make it to the left so that there is no chance of hitting Molly.*

Longarm squeezed off the first round, and it was a full second or two before he saw Molly's tormentor stiffen and then slap at his kidney. The big man goose-stepped away from Molly and then screamed something up at rim a moment before he toppled, rolled over twice and lay still.

"Gotcha, you sonofabitch!" Longarm whispered, as he levered out the spent cartridge and slammed in a fresh replacement. He took careful aim on a second outlaw and fired in one smooth, efficient killing motion.

Longarm and the Spencer were perfection because the number-two target also went down kicking and thrashing. Longarm quickly reloaded, but the others had scattered for cover, leaving Molly and the two dead outlaws in plain view.

"Yahoo!" Longarm shouted, jumping to his feet and waving his hat. He wasn't worried because they couldn't reach him with their piddling sidearms, and now it was his turn to do the taunting. "Come up here and get me, you bloody sonsabitches!"

He fired a couple more shots and then relaxed in plain view of the ranch house. Feeling better than he had all morning, Longarm stretched and extracted the stub of a cigar from his shirt pocket. Grinning wickedly, he lit it with the strike of a match and enjoyed the sharp bite of cigar smoke.

One by one, the outlaws emerged from hiding to stare up at him in stunned and hateful silence. Longarm waved at them, but they did not wave back. He chuckled, wondering how far Redbow had already descended. Given the half-breed's youth and agility, Longarm reckoned he might even be near the canyon floor by now.

"Come on!" he yelled, as the outlaws dragged the two dead men into the ranch house. "I'll be waiting right here for you!"

Moments later, two of the gang emerged with long rifles, maybe old buffalo rifles which Longarm figured would reach him with ease. Others sprinted out the back door for their horses and were soon flying out toward the canyon's mouth.

Longarm watched them separate into two groups and thought, *They'll be coming in at me from both sides of this mesa top. But it will take them at least two hours to get here, and by then I'll be down in their canyon with Molly and Redbow.*

Molly's head was turned up toward the rim, and Longarm waved and then took cover as the big rifles were brought into play. He did not actually hear the whistle of slugs passing by, but he heard one of them strike a nearby tree branch.

"Missed!" he shouted.

The second big-bore rifle thundered, and this time a slug whined close to his head. Longarm sat down in the rocks and enjoyed the remainder of his cigar. For the very first time, he was thinking that things might actually work out in their favor. Much of the outcome, of course, depended on Redbow. The day was still young, and the killing had just begun.

Where, he wondered, as he levered a fresh cartridge into the Spencer, *is that blood-lusting half-breed?*

Redbow could not believe that the marshal had managed to kill the leader of these men and one other member of the Four Corners Gang. It seemed impossible that a Spencer rifle could make such a long shot—but it had.

Now, as he hurried down the final few dozen yards and dove for cover behind the corral, he could hear Molly's groans and see her exposed white flesh bound to a corral pole.

"Molly!" he hissed. "It's Redbow! Can you see anyone watching you from inside the house?"

She didn't hear him, so he slithered into the corral, being careful not to get hung up with his bow and quiver of arrows. A moment later he was up and racing across the corral, scattering the frightened horses.

"Molly, it's all right," he whispered, kneeling behind her where he could not be seen from the house. "We're going to get you out of this right now!"

"Redbow?"

"None other," the half-breed whispered, dragging out his Bowie knife so that he could cut away the ropes that bound her so tightly. "Just don't move until I tell you, and then drop flat and I'll pull you back into the corral where we have cover."

"A few stayed behind to use me as a lure. If you cut the ropes, they'll open fire."

"If I leave you here like this, you're also dead."

A sob escaped Molly's swollen lips. Redbow couldn't see her face, but he knew that it was probably disfigured from the blows of the big man's fist. But now he had to make a decision: if Molly was right and she was bait, they'd kill her before he could drag her under the lowest pine pole of the corral fence. At this distance, and probably now armed with rifles, they would not miss.

What am I going to do?

"Molly, I'm going to sneak around the cabin and catch them by surprise. It's your only chance."

"Oh, gawd, I hurt so bad!"

"I'm going to kill every last one," Redbow hissed. "Or else they'll kill me."

"What about Curtis?"

"He's waiting for the ones that come up on top."

"Then he hasn't got a chance."

"Hang on, because this will be over soon one way or the other," Redbow told her before leaving.

Up on the mesa, Longarm's rifle barked three more times, and one of the shots shattered a rear window. Redbow heard cursing and figured he had best make use of this very timely distraction provided by the marshal. He ducked under the lowest rail, sprinted hard for a water trough and then made a running dive. No shots yet. Hadn't they seen him? Maybe they were all looking up at the rim or staying low in fear of a stray bullet. Whatever the reason, Redbow used it to his advantage as he jumped up and raced to the back of the house and began to edge around to the front where the outlaws would never anticipate an attack.

It would have helped very much to know how many men were in the house hoping to kill whomever came to Molly's rescue. And if time had not been so important, Redbow would have crept up to the front door, slipped inside and attempted to get both his bearings and a body count. But there was no time, so he nocked an arrow on his bowstring and started for the front door. His pistol and knife were in place, and he knew that he would have to use them fast . . . and well.

One of the gang rushed out the door, saw Redbow in the corner of his eye and tried to reverse his direction, but an arrow pierced his ribs and he collapsed, mouth distended with disbelief, a moment before Redbow's blade flashed and blood gushed from his severed throat. A moment later the half-breed was inside the ranch house with a pistol clenched in his fist.

"Do you see anybody comin' for her!" a voice shouted from the back of the building.

"No!"

"Sonofabitch! I say we ought to just kill her and go join the others. I don't like this one damned bit!"

"Me, neither. I'll put a slug right in her—"

Redbow's pistol barked three times, and then he ducked

sideways as the last living outlaw in the room returned fire. Redbow waited a second and then dropped and rolled back into the doorway, the muzzle of his gun flashing. The outlaw crashed up against the wall, fingers flailing helplessly at his riddled chest. Then he collapsed.

Redbow quickly reloaded. One of the outlaws was groaning and thrashing on the floor, making it impossible to hear if there was anyone else alive in the house. Redbow went over and silenced him with his already blood-wet blade.

He listened for the creak of floorboards or the heavy breathing of a man who feared dying. But there were no more sounds in the ranch house, so Redbow ran outside to free Molly.

When he saw her from the front, he had to still something inside him that rose up like poison in his throat. They'd beaten her face and lashed her body, probably with a quirt, until it was crisscrossed with bloody welts. Her mouth was a mass of blood, her eyes swollen almost completely shut so that she could not even see him as he ran to her side.

"We've got to move fast," Redbow told the woman as he wiped his knife blade clean on his pants. "We've got to get out of here."

She began to sob uncontrollably as he cut her free and then half-carried her into the house where he stripped an outlaw and covered her with his bloody clothes.

"Molly," he said, voice firm but gentle, "the marshal is up on the rim, and they're going after him. There are a lot of men up there now, so we need to signal him to come down quick."

"But then what do—"

"We must have horses saddled and ready to ride."

"But I can't even see" she told him, the words coming out wrong between her battered lips. "Redbow, I don't know . . ."

"Never mind," he said. "I'll stay with you except for when I'll need to catch and saddle us horses."

"How did you kill them all?"

"With pleasure," Redbow growled as he led her back toward the corral, supporting her with one arm and waving the other up at the rim to signal the marshal that it was time for all of them to move.

Chapter 19

Longarm had watched the half-breed emerge on the canyon floor and then go into action with a mixture of relief and admiration. From his vantage point high on the rim, he'd seen Redbow duck around to the front of the house and then kill one of the gang members with an arrow. During the next few tense moments, Custis had listened to muffled sounds of gunfire coming from the building and had been almost certain that Redbow was a dead man. But then, the amazing half-breed emerged and ran across the yard to untie poor Molly.

"That man is a killing machine," Longarm said to himself, "and I'm lucky that we're still on the same side of the law . . . I think."

When Redbow urgently beckoned him to climb down the steep, rocky cliff, Longarm's first thought was *hell no!* However, when he saw the glint of an outlaw's hatband concha and remembered that there were at least six of the Four Corners Gang hurrying to catch him in a deadly crossfire, he reconsidered.

"Here goes," Longarm sighed, as the first rifle shot off the mesa top sailed well overhead as he jumped over the edge.

Longarm dug his bootheels into the loose shale and

squatted as he began to sled downward at an increasing rate of speed. He came to a drop-off and went sailing into thin air but landed hard on his backside again, grabbing at bushes and scrub as he desperately attempted to slow his speed. Finally he struck an outcropping of rock, teetering precariously over a fifty-foot incline and holding on for dear life.

"Holy cow!" he swore, when he dared to open his eyes and assess his perilous predicament. "A damned mountain goat would break its damned neck trying to get down this cliff!"

He might even have begun to cuss at Redbow, except that a rifle slug fired from almost directly overhead kicked dirt into his face. Longarm had no choice but to roll onto his belly and slide. It seemed like he was in a complete free fall, and Longarm felt the front of his shirt and vest tear loose. Somehow he managed to hang onto his precious pocket watch and derringer as he began to tumble head over heels. His eyes filled with rock dust, and he felt as if his skin as being peeled away, which it probably was as he snowballed down completely out of control.

The little scrub pine that saved his life wasn't much to look at, just a runty thing that somehow clung to the cliff and jutted pathetically out into space. The force of Longarm's momentum wrapped his body around the pine like a piece of spaghetti; he momentarily lost consciousness as the air blasted from his lungs. He slipped off the rough bark and bounced on down the cliff until he landed on a loose shale rockslide, which he rode about a hundred yards before he crashed through a big manzanita patch. When he came out on the downside, his clothes were in tatters, and he somersaulted the remainder of the way on down to the canyon floor.

The half-breed had watched open-mouthed with astonishment and then ran to where Custis lay partially covered by loose shale. Digging him free, Redbow shouted, "Marshal! Are you alive?"

"Holy cow," Custis gasped. "I'm finally done for."

Redbow hauled him to his feet, and Longarm staggered into the ranch yard and over to a horse water trough.

"Climb in and you'll feel better," Redbow ordered. "I can't believe how clumsy you were coming down! What kind of a marshal are you, anyway?"

"A mostly dead one," Longarm mumbled, as he pitched headfirst into cold water.

He sank to the bottom, holding his breath, but inwardly screaming as his torn flesh burned. Longarm had been jumped a few times and beaten, but he'd *never* been so battered as he was right now. The only thing left on him was his boots, a few tattered pieces of his pants and an empty gunbelt.

"I don't think that either you or Molly are going to be much help." Redbow started to add something to that obvious fact, but the men on the ridge had reached Longarm's former, lofty position and were now beginning to open fire.

"Let's get out of here!" Redbow urged.

Somehow, they managed to climb on horseback after the half-breed had lead three animals around to the front of the house where the men on top could not get them in their rifle sights. Redbow led the two half-dead whites out of the canyon and then deposited them at its mouth and went galloping back to the house. Longarm was barely aware of what was going on because he was in such intense pain. Molly was in almost as bad a shape.

"I can't look as bad as you look," Custis said through his torn lips.

"You look far worse," she mumbled through her own battered and bruised lips.

"What's Redbow doing?"

"I don't know. Maybe he's climbing that cliff to kill the rest of them."

"Impossible."

She squinted through a slit in her left eye. "You think so?"

Longarm drew a deep, painful breath. At least he could see properly. "Well, maybe not."

It was so difficult to talk that they sat in silence, holding the reins of their mounts until Redbow returned about twenty minutes later with saddled horses and a bundle of outlaw rifles.

"I thought we needed these since you lost yours coming down the side of that mountain."

"It wasn't a mountainside," Longarm spat angrily, "it was a sheer *cliff!*"

"It's obvious that you don't have even a drop of Indian blood."

"I don't think I have *any* blood left," Longarm growled, looking down at his torso and thighs.

"Listen, Marshal, there are six men left up on the mesa top, and they'll be coming down soon. We have to kill them."

"Or arrest them."

"Kill them."

"Yes," Molly agreed. "They won't surrender. We have no choice."

Longarm stared at the high rim that formed a horseshoe around this hidden valley. "I have to ask them to surrender," he said. "I'm not going to just open fire and cut them down without giving them a chance to surrender."

"Do you think they'll give *us* a chance?" Redbow demanded.

Before Longarm could answer, Molly said, "We've come through so much, and they've killed so many. Custis, why risk everything now?"

It was all that Custis could do to climb back on his feet. He lifted his hands before his eyes and saw that they were a bloody, swollen mess. The miracle was that he'd not broken any bones, at least he didn't think he had, although he hurt so bad in so many places that he could not be certain.

"Look," he wearily argued, "I have to order them to drop their weapons before we open fire. But I'll let Redbow pick the spot, so that if they don't . . . well, they won't stand much of a chance. That's the best that I can do and, in clear conscience, remain a federal law officer.''

Longarm had lost his badge, but that didn't change the fact that he had sworn to uphold the law, which did not condone murder, no matter how dire the circumstances.

''Okay,'' Redbow told him. ''But if we fail, they'll kill Molly. Can you stand to know that in your dying moment?''

''We won't fail,'' Longarm answered. ''That much you have my word on.''

Redbow just looked at him briefly before he turned to the horses and began untying the rifles.

The six came down from the mesa on a narrow, winding footpath and were grouped in a tight bunch. No doubt they'd seen Longarm, Molly and Redbow race for the mouth of the canyon and were sure that they were alone. When Longarm and the half-breed stepped out from cover, the outlaws were caught flat-footed and in the open.

''Hands up!'' Custis called with a Winchester clenched in his rock-ruined fists. ''You're under arrest!''

They went for their guns, all but one. And when the smoke cleared, all six were dead except the single outlaw who'd tried to run and whom Redbow had shot through both buttocks. He was in intense pain, howling and screaming.

''You're going to make it,'' Longarm told him, ''and you can't hurt any worse than me or Molly. So shut the hell up!''

Redbow pushed his way between them, holding his Bowie knife. Before Longarm even realized what was happening, the half-breed grabbed the wounded outlaw by the hair, bent back his head and pressed his blade to the exposed flesh of his throat.

''No!'' Longarm bellowed, turning his gun on Redbow and cocking back the hammer.

"Where is Yancy and his murdering brother, Cletus?" Redbow demanded, ignoring Longarm.

"Go to hell!" their captive sobbed.

Redbow pressed his blade harder against the outlaw's throat, causing him to screech in terror and then beg, "No, for gawd's sake, please don't!"

"Drop the knife!" Longarm shouted.

"Not until he answers me."

"Drop it!"

"Shoot or shut up!" Redbow hissed, twisting the man's head back even farther. "One last time. Where are Yancy and Cletus Hooker?"

"They . . . they're coming here!"

"When?"

"Tomorrow."

"How many of the gang are with them?"

"Just Yancy, Cletus and maybe a couple more! I swear you already killed the rest of us!"

Redbow drew back his knife, then in a move so sudden that Longarm had to blink to be sure that he saw it happen, the half-breed sliced off the outlaw's nose and hurled it into the rocks.

"Oh my gawd!" the outlaw wailed, covering his badly disfigured face. "I'm dying!"

The pistol in Longarm's fist trembled as he gaped at the outlaw who was trying to cup the blood pouring from what remained of his nose. He then turned his attention to Redbow.

"What kind of man *are* you?"

"Doesn't your Holy Bible say an eye for an eye and a tooth for a tooth?"

"Yes, but . . ."

"You should have seen the Hopi girl on Second Mesa after they raped and then cut off *her* nose, Marshal."

Without another word, Redbow mounted his horse and rode back up the canyon. Longarm and Molly watched him release his horse in the corral and then sit down on the front porch.

"What is he doing?" Molly asked as the outlaw continued to scream.

"He's starting to wait for Yancy and the Hooker brothers."

"Then God help them all," Molly whispered. "So what are we going to do now?"

Longarm turned to stare at the outlaw. "I think we'd better try to keep him from bleeding to death, and then we have a choice of either leaving this place or going back and waiting for Yancy and his brothers to arrive."

"Could you just leave Redbow?"

"No," Longarm told her, "I could not. Not even after what I've just seen him do."

"I couldn't either," Molly said. "So let's see if we can patch us all up and go help him face those killers tomorrow."

Longarm took a deep breath. He looked down at the wounds covering his body, at Molly's battered face and, lastly, at the sobbing outlaw.

Maybe, he thought, *it's time that I found a new line of work.*

Chapter 20

A storm moved in from the north late that afternoon, and it began to rain hard by evening. After rummaging around in the ranch house, Longarm found a jar of medicinal salve and applied it liberally to his skinned body. After bandaging the wounded outlaw's face and buttocks, they locked him in the saddle room. It had quickly gotten tedious listening to his sobbing, and the sight of his face had been very troubling for both Longarm and Molly.

"Maybe they won't come," Molly opined as they sat on the small front porch and watched lightning cast jagged bolts across the darkening sky. "Maybe this weather will discourage the Hookers, and they'll stay wherever they are."

"Maybe," Longarm agreed.

"They'll come," Redbow told them an instant before a loud clap of thunder boomed up on the mesa top. "If not tomorrow or the next day, then the next, but they *will* have to come."

Longarm figured Redbow was right, and that the only thing to do now was to rest, wait and recover. He had been forced to rifle the pockets of the dead outlaws in order to find their names for official records. One of the men had carried a few cigars. They weren't very good ones, but he

176

lit one up now and smoked it thoughtfully. He was trying not to think about the upcoming showdown or how much he hurt—but it wasn't easy.

"Redbow," he asked, "assuming you aren't killed tomorrow or I don't have to arrest you for obstructing justice or outright murder, what will you do when this is finished?"

The half-breed shrugged. "I will go back to help Lucy and that man reach Flagstaff. After that, I go to the Hopi mesas."

"And stay there?"

"Maybe I will be asked to join a clan. I prefer to be a Bear Clan member, but the Snake Clan is good, too. It doesn't matter. I will farm the corn and hunt deer, sheep and rabbits."

"I find that difficult to believe," Longarm told the man. "I think you enjoy fighting and killing men."

Redbow had been whittling a stick, but now he calmly regarded Longarm. "You think wrong, Marshal. I have one last fight and then no more."

"That remains to be seen."

"I will kill Yancy Hooker." Redbow looked him straight in the eye. "Marshal, you can have his brothers."

"Thanks."

Molly took a deep breath and then sighed. "Could we finally talk about something besides killing?"

The two men lapsed into thoughtful silence. After he finished his cigar, Longarm went into one of the bedrooms and fell asleep wishing he had a bottle of whiskey, or at least some beer, to help ease his pain. There was a mirror on the wall, but he didn't have the heart to see what he looked like, all scraped to hell.

Molly and the half-breed remained on the porch and watched the fierce storm. Finally, she asked what had been nibbling at her mind. "Don't you feel any remorse or sadness about all the people you killed today? Or about the one whose nose you cut off?"

He didn't answer.

"Redbow, I asked you a straightforward question."

"I owe you nothing. You owe *me*, so don't ask no more."

"I do owe you my life. But I can't help but be curious about *your* life."

"It is not important."

"I disagree."

Redbow stood, stretched and went into the house. When Molly followed a short time later, the half-breed was already asleep on the big horsehide couch.

The next morning Longarm slept late and then got up and dressed in a dead outlaw's clothing. He limped out of his bedroom to the kitchen where he saw Molly sitting at the table. She looked up, smiled bravely through purple lips and said, "Custis, I made us coffee."

"Good." Custis looked around the room. "Where is Redbow?"

"He's out riding herd, tending to the grazing horses and the cattle."

"Why?"

"I suppose because he figures if someone isn't out there looking normal, Yancy and his brothers won't enter this canyon without their guns in their hands."

"Good point." Longarm took a gulp of the coffee. "Do I still look worse than you?"

"Oh, very much worse."

"That's what I was afraid of."

Longarm drank his coffee slowly, enjoying its bite and strength. It had been a lone time since they'd had coffee, and he found he'd missed it.

"Custis, what are you going to do about Redbow?"

"What do you mean, exactly?"

"He's waiting for them alone because he knows you'll try to arrest them. And, since he's sworn to kill Yancy on sight, he can't allow you to get in his way."

"Yes, I understand that."

Molly placed her hand on his scabby forearm. "I didn't sleep very well last night. I had this horrible vision of you trying to stop Redbow and then getting in a gunfight."

"Who won?"

"Be serious!"

"I am. And I actually had the same picture. I'd be the first to admit that it's a problem, all right."

"So how are you going to handle it?"

"It seems that Redbow has come up with the solution. I'll leave him alone. If Yancy, Cletus and a couple of others come, Redbow will have to hang back and let them enter the trap this canyon presents. Then, when they ride up to this house, I'll step outside with a rifle and—"

"No, we'll *both* step out with rifles."

"All right. Both of us. I'll tell them they are all under arrest, and if they choose not to surrender, they'll die."

"Just like that?"

"We'll have the element of surprise, unless Redbow is very foolish and tries to brace them all by himself."

"I'm afraid that's exactly what he will do."

"I'm not," Longarm told her. "Sure, he's filled with hatred and the need for revenge. But he also knows how dangerous they are and wants them punished. Dead, if possible, but at least in prison, bound for a hangman's noose. So he'll allow them past him into this canyon and the trap. And then, if you or I or both of us are killed, he'll be waiting to finish off any surviving Hooker."

Molly refilled his coffee. "You know," she said with a lopsided smile, "we both look so terrible that the Hookers might just take one look at us and die of fright!"

It was meant to be a joke, but when Longarm tried to laugh, his face was so brittle and covered with scabs that it hurt.

"Let's just let this play out," he told Molly. "We can rest and get ready for the showdown. And every day we have to wait, we'll be that much stronger."

"All right," she agreed. "I found bacon and potatoes. How would you like a big, hot breakfast?"

"I'd like that fine, and if I had a glass of good whiskey to wash it down with and help ease my pains . . . no, on second thought, I'd better not. They just might arrive today like that noseless fella said."

At the mention of their captive, Molly's eyes filled with tears. "I can't imagine going through life without a nose. What—"

"Don't even think about it," Custis warned. "It won't help and can only hurt you."

They were sitting on the porch late that afternoon when they saw Redbow suddenly race his horse into the farthest animals belonging to the cattle herd. The half-breed looked back at them, and although he dared not signal, Longarm knew that the Hooker brothers, last survivors of the infamous Four Corners Gang, had arrived on schedule.

"Let's go inside and arm ourselves," he told Molly.

"I'm so glad that I found a shotgun. As scared as I am, I'm afraid I might miss with a pistol or rifle."

"Two barrels and the range will be perfect," Longarm told her. "You can't miss."

"But what if I accidentally hit and kill their horses!"

"Molly, the worst thing about you is that you worry far too much."

"So what do you think is the *best* thing about me?"

"I'll give it some thought later."

Because Longarm expected that the unsuspecting Hooker men would come right up to the hitching rail, he figured he would be best served with revolvers. He had found a gunbelt and holster, which would carry his backup revolver. The other he would have in his fist when he stepped outside to make his arrest. Now, he checked both pistols one last time and looked at Molly, who held the double-barreled shotgun.

"Are you all right?" he asked. "Because if you have

any doubts about your ability to see this through, then stay inside and blast anyone that I can't kill.''

''No, I'll be standing with you to the very end.''

''Okay then,'' he said, going over to the window. ''I count four . . . five.''

She took a deep, ragged breath and exhaled slowly. ''That's more than I thought.''

''Me, too,'' Longarm said, relaxing on the horsehide sofa and closing his eyes. ''Just be calm, and when you open fire with those twin cannons, be very deliberate and don't rush the shots.''

''Whatever you say,'' Molly whispered, coming over to sit close beside him these last few moments before the showdown.

It seemed like forever before they heard the jingle of spurs and the snort of a horse. Longarm suddenly pushed himself up and limped outside with Molly on his heels.

Yancy Hooker was half in and half out of his saddle when Longarm raised his gun and shouted, ''You're all under federal arrest! Hands up!''

The Hookers were all big, dark-complected and brutish men. They stared at Longarm and Molly as if they were witnessing two corpses which had just been hauled out of their graves.

''Who the hell are *you!*'' Yancy bellowed.

Before Longarm could reply, the noseless man in the saddle shop burst through a loose board in the wall. Maybe he'd pried it open during the night and had been waiting for just this moment, and when he ran out into the yard, he screamed, ''They cut off my nose, and they're gonna kill us all, Yancy!''

That was the spark that ignited the deadly explosion that now swept over them all. Longarm shot Yancy, but his slug was partially deflected by the man's saddlehorn. Yancy's horse reared, saving him from a second, fatal bullet, and then Longarm had no choice but to shift his aim to the others and try to take out as many as he could before they returned fire.

The tremendous boom of Molly's double shotgun blasts swept across the porch and nearly beheaded two of the outlaws. The third outlaw caught just the edge of the blast pattern, but that was enough to spin him completely out of his saddle. He landed and managed to fire, but a horse kicked him, and then Longarm drilled him through the forehead.

"Yancy is getting away!" Molly cried.

"No he's not," Longarm said, watching as Redbow raced his pony into the path of the wounded outlaw leader.

Longarm expected the half-breed to cut the big man down in a volley of gunfire, but Redbow jumped from his horse and fit an arrow onto his bowstring. Yancy was bent over and maybe even dying, but he still managed to raise his pistol and get off two shots before Redbow's arrow struck him in the neck.

"Oh my gawd!" Molly whispered as the outlaw leader slumped over his racing horse. As it swept by, Redbow jumped up high into the air and grabbed the heavy man by the arm, jerking him to the earth.

"I hope he's already dead!" Molly cried.

Redbow landed on Yancy's chest. Longarm caught a sudden glint of his knife blade, and then he heard Yancy begin to scream.

"What's—"

"You don't want to know, Molly. Just go inside!"

"But . . ."

Yancy's shriek filled the valley, and as he turned Molly away, Longarm saw Redbow lift the dying man's scalp and shake his long black hair like a banner.

They left the canyon without much to say except a simple good-bye. Longarm and Molly headed for Cortez with the bodies of the Four Corners Gang draped over the backs of a string of horses. Redbow, with his bloody trophy tied to his belt, headed south to fulfill his promise to help Lucy and Andy Drew.

"Do you think he'll really stop killing men?" Molly asked sometime the following day.

"Do you?"

"Yes."

Longarm nodded. "Molly, you're a worrier but also an incurable optimist, and that's the thing I like best about you."

She managed to smile. "When we're healed up a little, I'm going to tell you what I like best about *you*, Custis."

"Oh yeah? And what would that be?"

"Well, when you tumbled down that cliff, I was sure hoping that at least one big and important part of you was unharmed."

It hurt, but Longarm laughed anyway.

J. R. ROBERTS
THE GUNSMITH